THE SCARLET
LETTER SOCIETY

THE SCARLET LETTER SOCIETY

MARY T. McCARTHY

The following is a work of fiction. Names, characters, places, events and incidents are either the product of the author's imagination or used in an entirely fictitious manner. Any resemblance to actual persons, living or dead, is entirely coincidental.

ISBN 978-1-940610-39-9
eISBN 978-1-940610-29-0

First digital edition: June 2014 by Polis Books, LLC
First Trade Paperback edition: May 2015 by Polis Books, LLC
1201 Hudson Street
Hoboken, NJ 07030
www.PolisBooks.com

POLIS BOOKS

For my beloved sister Beth

"She had not known the weight until she felt the freedom."

The Scarlet Letter, Nathaniel Hawthorne

April 2012

It's throat-numbing spray," she grinned mischievously. "For blowjobs."

Eva Bradley, a petite woman in her early forties with neatly bobbed black hair, wore her standard issue corporate attorney Ann Taylor black pantsuit and brightly colored scarf du jour. She'd taken a small box from her Coach purse, removed a brown bottle, and placed it in the middle of the coffee shop's table with a dramatic, near jazz-hands-level flourish.

The small glass bottle landed — *thonk* — in the middle of the monthly invitation, accidentally hitting a bullseye on the standard giant red letter "A" watermarked on the page.

**"But he knows where she's goin' as she's leavin'
She's headed for the cheatin' side of town."
-"Lyin' Eyes," The Eagles**

Monthly meeting of the Scarlet Letter Society
Zoomdweebies Café
Friday, April 6, 2012
5:30 a.m.
"The scarlet letter was her passport into regions where
other women dared not tread."
-The Scarlet Letter, **Nathaniel Hawthorne**

Lisa always printed out the invite, which featured the same book quote at the bottom and a different song lyric each month. Scarlet Letter Society membership was exclusive, right now limited to only three women: Eva, Maggie and Lisa. The club bore the name of the literary bible of adultery: Nathaniel Hawthorne's *The Scarlet Letter*.

Glancing at the mysterious bottle, Maggie laughed. Next to her Lisa gaped, widening her chocolate-brown eyes; wrinkles instantly rippled like the international symbol for 'bacon' across her bewildered forehead.

Maggie Hanson, who owned the vintage clothing shop next door to the café where the women met, picked up the box. "Comfortably Numb," she read in her thick Boston accent, still smirking. "Well, that's a good a name as any for a blow job spray. Says here, '*the refreshing spritz contains a mild numbing element to coat the back of the throat, suppressing gag reflex during oral sex.*'"

Eva picked up the bottle, adding in a sing-songy ad-jingle voice, "Discreet enough to take with you wherever you go!

Doubles as a breath freshener!"

"Where the heck are you going?" said local bakery owner Lisa Swain, looking completely stupefied as she glanced at the flavor on the package: Chocolate Mint.

"It comes in *flavors*?" she asked, her usually pale face beet red against her light blonde hair.

Eva smiled. "Of course. Like at the dentist!"

Maggie raised her eyebrows at Lisa and told her, "You know, this stuff works better when guys use it."

Eva rolled her eyes. "Is that what all your gay best friends tell you?"

Maggie replied, "No, smarty pants. I mean if you spray it on your man's fundangles, it takes him longer to come. Also, his junk is now a chocolate mint lollipop. Everyone's a winner."

"I planned on using it for an upcoming meeting in DC," said Eva sheepishly, a sexy twinkle in her eye.

Maggie nodded knowingly. "Hopefully not *during* the meeting, ya big whore. Let me guess," she said. "Late night meeting with your intern, Ron?"

Lisa chimed in, "Honestly, Eva, I can't believe you're sleeping with someone who was born in the 1980s. He was named after Ronald Reagan, for the love of God! And you were in high school then!"

"Technically, I was only in 8th grade when he was born." Eva blushed. "I mean, it's not like I'm old enough to be his mom or anything."

Maggie added, "Yeah, unless you were one hell of a slutty 8ᵗʰ grader. Did they have chocolate mint blow job spray back then, Mrs. Robinson?"

All three ladies laughed. Lisa took a sip of her iced coffee drink and pointed out,

"I picked a really awkward day for a mint mocha latte."

"GOOD MORNING, Tara," said Zarina Harandi. Zarina owned Zoomdweebies, a popular indie bookshop café in Keytown, Maryland, the state's second-largest city.

"So happy to be here." said Tara. "I was looking for a copy of the new Stephen King book, and then, of course, the *Baltimore Sun.*"

"Of course," said Zarina, walking across the worn wood floors. The shop was painted in 80s classic bright yellow to match its vintage pride and joy, a Ms. Pac Man arcade game.

"You never have to worry about the battery dying on a book," said Tara.

"True," said Zarina. Her mother Kate had opened this shop after her dad, an Iranian immigrant, died six years before. Kate founded the shop because, she said, "Women need a place to circle their wagons— even if their wagons come in the form of minivans." Kate was an 80s girl to the max, thus the inspiration for the shop name, Zoomdweebies, a reference to the Judd-Nelson-as-John-Bender character from the 1985 John Hughes film *The Breakfast Club.*

"And not surprisingly, I'll have my usual," said Tara, smiling. Zarina knew that was a double shot espresso iced latte with skim milk and a shot of vanilla.

"Coming right up," said Zarina.

"What would this town do without your shop?" said Tara. "I don't want to live in a world where you can't still walk somewhere to buy a book, coffee and a paper."

"Me either," said Zarina. She'd finished college the year before, returning home to run the coffee shop when her mom began working as a professor at the local university. Not knowing what she wanted to do with her Journalism degree, she figured running Zoomdweebies was as good an idea as any for the moment.

Besides, she liked it here. Her seemingly quiet personality allowed her to fade into the background to a point where people forgot she was there. But huddled over a laptop at a small desk in the corner of the shop behind the counter in-between making avocado and Brie wraps and nonfat chai lattes? Like the janitor in *The Breakfast Club*, she heard and saw everything.

Tara thanked Zarina for the coffee and settled into a cozy, worn red velvet chair to read her paper. Zarina knew Tara only had a short time before she had to go pick up her preschooler.

Next to Tara, *Pretty in Pink* played silently on a vintage TV and VHS player. *"Wonder whatever happened to Jake Ryan after that movie?"* Tara pondered when she saw it playing.

"Bet he's still hot." The shop played an endless series of 80s movies on VHS: *Ferris Bueller's Day Off, Stripes, Ghostbusters, Sixteen Candles, Caddyshack,* and the stacks went on and on. Kate found the entire VH1 series of "I Love the 80s" and had it converted backwards from digital into VHS tapes by some local hipster geek who told her, *"Excellent choice in formats, dude."*

Tara and the shop's other regular customers loved the movies playing in the background, often turning up the volume to watch a scene or two. It was always the cool people who gathered around to watch the Carl Spackler "Cinderella story" scene from *Caddyshack* and asked to turn the volume up. Those were the customers Zarina wanted as regulars, not the uptight, pantyhose-wearing mothers who demanded *Airplane* be turned off when Captain Oveur asks Joey if he's ever seen a grown man naked.

Those bitches can go to Starbucks, Zarina had thought.

All kinds of people came into the café. As a journalist, Zarina kept a notebook to write character sketches for future stories. There was a husband and wife who stopped by every Tuesday morning and ordered exactly the same thing. *Only they're on their way to marriage counseling,* thought Zarina. There was a teenage boy who came in at the same time after school every day, buying only a bag of Mystery flavor Air Heads. *He's only here because he hopes the blonde lacrosse player will come in with her friends to giggle over skim mochaccinos.*

And there were the moms. Although occasionally there

was the lone mom like Tara, who came in to actually read a book and get some peace and quiet while her child was at school, most of the moms travelled in gaggles, like geese. There were PTA moms (the most annoying; the way they yammered on about cookie dough fundraisers and teacher appreciation donuts made Zarina's head spin), save-the-planet moms (cloth diapers, raw organic homemade baby food), and brand new moms (dark circles and sweatpants) just trying to have human contact with someone other than a newborn.

Thinking of the early morning visit of the adulteresses, Zarina smiled at the thought of someone like Tara overhearing a conversation about blowjob spray.

"*'Adultresses' seems like an outrageously old-fashioned word to use,*" Zarina thought, as she cleaned the espresso maker, "*but what else is there to call them? The Women Who Cheat on Their Husbands? MILFs?*" Some would say 'sluts' or 'whores' in a more serious way than the club members, who used the terms jokingly. "*Maybe it's best to just call them what they call themselves, in honor of Nathaniel Hawthorne's famous novel,*" Zarina decided. They're simply known as "The Scarlet Letter Society."

"I DON'T know what I'd do if Ron and Charles found out about each other," whispered Eva after the gathering at the coffee shop. "Not to mention if my husband found out about my two lovers. Ugh."

The worn oval sign reading *Wings Vintage Clothing* creaked on its iron hinges as the women entered Maggie's downtown shop, its name chosen as a tribute to her favorite piece of literature, Erica Jong's revolutionary 1973 book *Fear of Flying*. Maggie had even gone so far as to name her first daughter Erica (her other daughter's name, Lilith, also reflected a healthy sense of feminism.)

"Well it's plenty to worry about, hussy," laughed Maggie. She tossed her unruly reddish-brown curls, always bordering on disheveled and frizzy, over her shoulders. The two had been friends for years and shared the comfortable conversation style reserved for sisterhood and rare relationships between women.

Eva absentmindedly dusted the top of a vintage frame containing a piece of antique handmade needlework that served as another nod to the shop name: *"My child, I wish you two things. To give you roots, and to give you wings."*

"I need advice," declared Eva. "Everything is just so complicated, and I honestly feel like my life is spinning way out of control. Have you ever felt that way?"

Maggie smiled, a glint in her green eyes. "Yeah, once upon a time, I guess I did."

Eva replied, "Well, what did you do? I feel like my whole life is a circus, and I'm a terrible ringleader."

Maggie turned to face Eva. "You just gotta learn how to keep all the balls in the air."

"There are just so many balls!" said Eva. Both women laughed. "Now help me pick out something vintage and fabulous to wear to my meeting next week."

Maggie picked out a few vintage 40s dresses and sent Eva into a dressing room. Eva modeled; everything always looked amazing on her. Maggie rang up the purchase, sending Eva on her way with a hug, some reassurance to take one day at a time, and an A-line navy dress that looked stunning on her petite frame.

As she put the dress into a bag, a certain smell triggered a long ago memory. After Eva left the shop, Maggie sat in a trance-like state, remembering.

Frost formed on the insides of the two-room efficiency apartment window. Maggie was locked inside alone on one of many nights when her mother, a waitress at a nearby bar, couldn't afford a sitter. Maggie didn't even remember her own mother's name, only that she'd run home to check on her only child during fifteen-minute breaks, smelling of stale cigarettes and beer. Like a choppy scene from a horror movie, the images flickering and jerky and too quick, then too slow, then too quick, Maggie thought of nights where her mother tucked her into bed, leaving a flashlight on the nightstand in case she had to use the bathroom. The electric bill hadn't been paid. The smell. That familiar smell, from the hourglass-shaped glass bottle with the gold bow. Her mother would spray that Estee Lauder (a gift, somehow Maggie knew it had been a gift... but from who?) on her to hide the bar smells before she climbed into bed with Maggie; they'd slept in the same bed to stay warm.

The jingle of the shop door's bell jolted Maggie back into the moment, her face flushed and hands sweaty. Her heart was beating faster and her head was pounding as she reached for the pills in her purse.

"Daymares?"

It was Dave, Maggie's first husband, who knew she called her daytime trances "daymares" since they reminded her of nightmares.

Maggie's face softened when she saw Dave: bearded, tall, corduroy and flannel-clad. He walked over and hugged her.

EVA COULDN'T get the lyrics to "Lyin' Eyes" out of her head ever since Maggie had sent the invite to that month's Scarlet Letter Society meeting. The line *"she's so far gone, she feels just like a fool"* played in her head after she left Maggie's shop and headed over the Chesapeake Bay Bridge toward her mother's Matthew's Island cottage on what James Michener called "the calmer waters of the Eastern Shore" of Maryland.

Her phone rang as she finished crossing the bridge, and *"Call from Ron"* appeared on her car dashboard screen. She answered it on the steering wheel of her Mars Red Mercedes SLK 350 Roadster.

"Eva Bradley," she crooned in a fake professional tone as she answered the phone.

"Ms. Bradley, this is your intern Ron. I'm calling to let you know that your meeting next Thursday morning meeting needs to be rescheduled due to a conflict with the client."

"Ron, you're my only intern at the moment. You don't have to introduce yourself. You can call and tell that particular client to gargle my balls, because this is the third time she's canceled."

A moment's pause. "Er, Ms. Bradley, I'm not sure the phrase 'gargle my balls' is one that the madam Fortune 500 executive is used to hearing..."

Eva laughed. "I've been hanging around Maggie too much. Well, I'll leave it to you to phrase that in a more diplomatic way, then, Ron. In the meantime, I demand to know why your body is not underneath mine right now."

"Ms. Bradley, are you driving?"

"Yes, Ron, I am."

"Well then, the answer is that I wouldn't want to wreck a perfectly gorgeous piece of German machinery. I will, however, be happy to fill your empty appointment slot on Thursday morning since your client canceled."

"In that case," replied Eva, blushing slightly despite herself and snickering, "you can thank that bitch of a client for me."

Eva hung up the phone, smiling at the way her body tingled just hearing her young lover's voice. He made her happy. Her husband Joe, a department head physician at Johns Hopkins University in Baltimore, worked virtually 24-7. Her twin boys Calvin and Graham were fourteen, started high school this year, and were hormonal and smelly and awful. She loved her family like crazy, but escaping from them seemed to be all she ever wanted to do—which of course brought on guilt, because she was raised Catholic, and if anyone could send you on an all-expenses paid mom-guilt trip to the moon and back any day of the week, it was the Catholics.

She had somehow managed to position herself to be a forty-one-year-old woman who was cheating on both her forty-five-year-old husband and her fifty-three-year-old lover with her twenty-eight-year-old intern. Her sex drive aside, it was Eva's workaholism that really drove her. Her career as a corporate attorney was both successful and demanding, and she often wondered if all the steam she put into the corporate machine during her long workweeks was exactly the steam she was blowing off with her various creative sexual outlets.

Suddenly the phone rang again.

Without looking at the dashboard, Eva purred, "How may I help you?" in a seductive voice.

"EEE-vah?" asked her husband, Joe. Her name was pronounced "ee-vah" though people often mispronounced it "Ay-va." When Joe thundered the word, the first half sounded like it was being shouted in a capital letter: *EEE-vah.*

Eva was snapped back into her reality like a branch in a thunderstorm. She unknowingly shifted her driving position. Where she had been reclining back into her leather seats, sunroof open, hair blowing in the wind, she now sat upright, straightened and stiffened. "Hey Joe," Eva replied, trying to sound casual. "What's up?"

"What's up is that your sons just got busted behind the school football field bleachers drinking beers."

Eva winced at the way Joe referred to their sons when they were in trouble, as "your sons." When they made state championship teams in lacrosse, he called them "my boys."

Joe continued. "Apparently you didn't answer your cell phone, so the Vice Principal Ken Tracey called me to let me know they were suspended for three days. And that was after I spent fifteen minutes convincing him that they shouldn't be expelled. So fortunately, they will make it through at least their first year of high school."

Eva cringed. Dreaded, ever-present mommy guilt immediately flared up. Somehow, it was her fault. She traveled too much and the boys were acting out in rebellion. Now they would do terribly in high school and then not get into good colleges. And all of that was because their mother was a wine drinking, career-obsessed sex freak and their father worked all the time.

Eva cleared her head, and her throat, and responded, "What should we do about OUR sons?" She hated how she sounded. She couldn't understand how she could ruin entire corporations in the courtroom without batting an eyelash, but when it came to dealing with her husband, she turned into a handkerchief-gripping 1950s housewife, complete with red and white checked apron.

Joe replied, "Destroy their lives as they know them?"

Eva sighed. "Have you spoken to them? What's the rest of the story? Some older kid must've given them the beer. This is the first time they've done anything like this. We should sit down as a family and discuss it."

Joe bellowed, "The rest of the story? There is no rest of the story. I sent them to their rooms for the weekend. I don't want to see their faces."

"So you didn't talk to them?" inquired Eva, marveling at the fact that all her husband, a pediatric oncologist at one of the top medical institutions in the country, could muster up when the first sign of teen angst acting out appeared was a big time out chair.

"There is nothing to say," said Joe. "You can come home and deal with them."

Eva had already been debating doing a U-turn on Kent Island to head back to the Western Shore of Maryland. But this was *her weekend*. She hadn't been to the island in a month, had promised her mother a visit, and she couldn't travel there again for at least another month. Her mother honestly needed her.

"I'll just spend one night with Mom," said Eva, compromising. "Tomorrow when I get home, I will speak with the boys, and I'll text them tonight."

Joe laughed.

"Why would you think they would still have phones?" He hung up.

Eva winced and began the inevitable beating-herself-up

routine. Although their father was emotionally vacant from their boys' lives, preferring to lose himself in his work than to take his own sons to an Orioles game, Eva still blamed herself when there was a low grade on a test or a small altercation on the lacrosse field.

Eva pulled her car over to get an iced coffee; she'd need it to get through this drive. She opened the Facebook application on her iPhone. Her husband wouldn't realize it, but she knew the boys were fully technologically functioning without the phones. The spoiled brats each had MacBooks and iPads in their rooms, and even Internet through the Wiis on their bedroom TVs.

She wanted to cyberstalk them a tiny bit, just a quick check of Facebook pages, to be sure they weren't bragging about their exploits. She private messaged both of them in the same message on Facebook.

Dear Graham and Calvin,

Nice job, boys. Dad's pissed and I can't exactly say I'm a proud mom. Do not use your Facebook accounts. If I see any use on them, I'll disable them. The last thing you need is to mess up your college chances by bragging about your little escapades. I will be home tomorrow and we can discuss this. In the meantime, be productive. Do homework! Clean your rooms! Do dishes! Don't leave the house.

*Spend time thinking about how stupid of a decision
you just made and how incredibly crappy your
summer is going to be because of it.*

*Hugs,
Mom*

Eva sipped her coffee and pulled back onto Rt. 50. A
quick visit to the island was just what she needed. Watching
the sun set over the bay would help recharge her batteries for
having to deal with the boys tomorrow.

Motherhood really sucks sometimes, she thought.
Hollywood's version—all fluffy blankets and cute messy
banana-eating baby faces and angelic three-year-old
handprint molds—comprised about 10% of being a mother.
The other 90% was temper tantrums and math homework
you couldn't understand and dealing with bickering and
nagging about messy rooms and piles and piles of laundry
that went on forever, because it didn't ever end. *The. Laundry.
Never. Ends.*

Eva wanted to send out a public service announcement
for women who, like Lisa, were struggling with infertility:

*Hey, gals! Don't feel bad about being childless! Wanna know a
huge secret that moms never talk about, because it would make us
realize how miserable we really are a lot of the time? IT SUCKS!
Your life is OVER! Forget sleep! Stay home with them and you're
broke! Go back to work and feel guilty, PLUS spend a fortune on*

childcare! You can't take a shower for more than three consecutive minutes over the next eighteen years! You're going to eat crap because kids eat macaroni and cheese and chicken nuggets, not shrimp scampi and filet mignon! Time for you to go to the gym or read a book? Forget it. Your sex life? OVER! With your husbands, anyway...

Boy, that would be a popular article, wouldn't it?

She shook her head and headed southeast.

EARLY SCARLET Letter Society meeting times worked well for Lisa, because she could attend the gatherings before she opened her bakery. Her husband Jim was a real estate developer in DC, and his long commute made for lonely mornings to kill in their suburban subdivision.

Lisa flipped open her laptop.

Her email contained the usual junk mail, two pie orders, and the one she was looking for—a note from her graphic designer and crush, Ben. She blushed in anticipation and shame.

from: **Ben** bnidale@starfishdesign.com
to: **Lisa** lswain@blackbirdspie.com

date: Monday, April 9, 2012, 5:36 AM

subject: Good morning

> Good morning, lovely baker. I hope your
> day is awesome. Your email came just as
> I was thinking about you. See you Friday
> for pie meeting…if not before.

> Ben

Lisa grinned.

Blackbirds Pie was a few blocks away from the coffee shop. She had met Ben when she hired his downtown advertising agency to design a new logo and he was assigned to be her graphic designer. At thirty-seven and wanting a baby, she hadn't been out looking to complicate her life with an affair.

It was that simple, she thought now, warding off thoughts of how complicated it was. *We just really like each other and we have fun together.* Lisa could hear the replay in her head as she told the other women her story at the meeting a few months back.

"So what's your story, newbie?" Maggie had demanded, by way of welcoming the new member to the club.

"Well," Lisa had begun, awkwardly. "Ben is just so sweet and attentive. One day we were having a lunch meeting and drank too much wine and we just ended up totally going at it on the Pier One Imports wicker couch in the back office of my bakery."

Eva and Maggie had laughed, so Lisa, grabbing at the

skin of her neck absentmindedly with one hand, continued.

"Ben threw me up against the small walk-in freezer," she embellished. "We had our tongues halfway down each other's throats and we couldn't get our clothes off fast enough." She paused. "Don't ask me why, but he grabbed a jar of cherries off the shelf as we made our way to my office. We fed each other maraschino cherries while we made out. Cherry juice dripped everywhere."

She finished the story by reporting that she had already replaced the old couch, which had been both uncomfortable and irreversibly stained with cherry juice.

Recalling it, Lisa's smile fell. Only she knew that the story was all a lie, a complete and utter fabrication.

The fictionalized account seemed realistic enough. Lisa didn't know what to do to stop her unrelenting crush on Ben, and wasn't sure she wanted it to stop. It had only been a few short months since they met. But they hadn't so much as kissed, much less drowned each other in any kind of juices.

Lisa had lied her way in to the Scarlet Letter Society.

If the women in the club knew she hadn't actually cheated on her husband, she would have been disinvited from her membership. She felt awful deceiving them, but when Maggie and Eva had visited her bakery one day and she overheard their discussion, she was overcome with curiosity about how they got away with their affairs. The two women had mentioned their third club member moving away, and Lisa had swallowed down her shyness and asked if she could join them for coffee.

Her five-year marriage hadn't been particularly miserable, and she loved her husband. Something was just…missing.

Better Out Than In, she'd written on page one of her current journal — she'd kept one all her life. The worn leather journal, tucked away in its floral Vera Bradley case, knew that her marriage's main frustration centered on the couple's inability to get pregnant. But running a business was exhausting and lonely. While she and Ben had started out in a professional relationship that grew into a friendship, the mutual flirtation seemed to grow stronger each day.

She glanced at the current (and original) Pottery Barn couch, warming at the memory of the last day she'd seen Ben as she hit "reply":

> from: **Lisa** lswain@blackbirdspie.com
> to: **Ben** bnidale@starfishdesign.com
>
> date: Monday, April 9, 2012 at 1:10 PM
> subject: Earlybird
>
> You were up early sending email, mister! Busy day, just getting to my inbox. Yes. Friday. Pie. Can't wait. Will have your favorite flavor ready.
> ☺ L

Lisa wasn't sure she knew exactly how she'd become

such a flirt. From an early age, she had always been reserved. She was prettier than average, though not beautiful; tall, thin, her dark brown eyes exuding inner strength despite uncertainty. She usually dashed on some quick foundation powder, mascara and lip gloss, but only on shop days.

Her husband's dominant personality was one of the things that had first drawn her to him—she wanted someone else to be in charge of her life. After they'd met at a Chamber of Commerce event six years ago, Jim's confidence had won her over and although she never really felt like she was head over heels in love with him, she'd made the thirty-two-year-old-ticking-biological-clock decision to marry him when he asked her, simply because he seemed to need her. A half decade in, and now that she was running a successful business, his domineering persona got on her nerves more than anything. That, and his goddamned obsessive foot fetish.

The foot fetish had been a favorite topic at Scarlet Letter Society meetings. And it was funny, sort of, except for the part that it was actually happening to her.

Should I or shouldn't I? Lisa wrote, and closed the journal, tucking it away in its case inside her purse.

HER COMBINATION island/home discipline weekend behind her, Eva was back in New York. She woke up from a deep sleep to find a tongue inside her. An unshaven face with its perfect two-day growth gently scratched the insides of her thighs as she arched her back. She clutched the pillow beside her and whispered, "Good morning to you, too, sir."

His smile touched the most intimate parts of her, and she laughed at the sensation of his chin stubble. He didn't stray from his task, expertly holding down her upper thighs with his forearms, demanding that she relinquish control to him. It wasn't something she was used to. In all other parts of her life, if she had nothing else, she had control. There was a reason her name was on the door of the law firm perched high in the Manhattan skyline. It was no accident she was at the top.

In fact, she recalled now, she preferred to be on top. She squeezed her toned inner thighs together, planning to flip this horny chef onto his back so she could have her own way with him.

He was having none of it. His hours at the gym weren't spent there just so he could lift cast iron pans. He now incorporated his broad, strong legs to encircle her feet. She wasn't going anywhere.

She knew from experience that she may as well prop a pillow under her head, relax every muscle in her body, and enjoy the ride. As he rotated his tongue, his thumb gently caressed her. In a matter of minutes, she exploded in a powerful, sweet orgasm that left her body quivering.

His dark, curly, grinning head appeared from under the sheet. He was completely naked, his erection rising to greet her. And then suddenly, the expression on his face turned to horror.

"Oh my gosh, madame," the man uttered in his heavy French accent. "*Je regrette!* I am so sorry. I thought you were someone else. I must have the wrong hotel room. This is so embarrassing."

He hopped out of bed, grabbing his pants and practically running in circles to collect his belongings.

Eva lay on the bed and laughed heartily, her hand over her mouth.

"Well, to be honest with you, monsieur, I'm not sure whose hotel room you're supposed to be in, but I wish you would stay in this one."

Charles tossed his clothes playfully into the air and plopped himself naked onto the bed.

"Well in that case, madame, I'm here to serve."

Eva laughed again. She honestly believed that half the reason she was having this insane, delicious affair in the first place was Charles's sense of humor. He could always make her laugh. Not just laugh, but laugh from the belly, when you can't stop yourself no matter how hard you try. Such laughter was so rare in her life.

He was the head chef at The Plaza Hotel, where she stayed a few times a month on business at the firm. Her DC office was where she normally worked, but these visits to New York were her favorite part of the month.

Charles sat up in the bed, leaned down, cupped her

face into his capable hands, and kissed her slowly, gently, passionately.

She kissed him back, the tingle in her spine working its way to every part of her being. Though she had already had an earth-shaking orgasm, her body was hungry for more. She wanted him inside her.

Eva felt Charles' growing erection as it grazed her silk chemise. Her panties were already gone, apparently removed while she slept. She smiled at the thought. His hunger for her was insatiable.

She grabbed his strong shoulders, pulling him into her embrace, returning his eager kisses, a soft moan parting her lips as she anticipated what would follow. She reached down to stroke him as he made a motion to climb on top of her. His fingers gently but decisively found their mark between her legs.

"Not this time," Eva whispered, rising up from the bed and in a single motion circling herself up and over onto all fours, straddling him. They both smiled. It was her turn to be in control.

May 2012

"I'm your hell, I'm your dream. I'm nothing in between.
You know you wouldn't want it any other way."
— "Bitch," Meredith Brooks

Monthly meeting of the Scarlet Letter Society
Zoomdweebies Café
Friday, May 4, 2012
5:30 a.m.

"The scarlet letter was her passport into regions where
other women dared not tread."
-*The Scarlet Letter*, Nathaniel Hawthorne

from: **Maggie** mags@wingsvintage.com

to: lswain@blackbirdspie.com, embradley@smithcohenbradley.com

date: Tuesday, May 1, 2012 at 10:26 AM

subject: Happy May Day, SLS!

Greetings, SLutS!

It's that time again. Attached is your invitation to this month's meeting of the Scarlet Letter Society. Don't forget, next month will be our first book club discussion of *The Scarlet Letter* by Nathaniel Hawthorne. So don't forget to pick up your copy from Zarina if you haven't already. See you Friday!

Scarlet Letter Society meetings were held monthly when the combination coffee shop/bookstore was closed, always at the same time: first Friday of the month, 5:30 am.

Comfy in her standard attire--a vintage t-shirt (today: Smurfs) and worn jeans--Maggie flopped into the orange 70s vinyl recliner. Maggie smiled, remembering the day she crammed the chair into the back of her '09 Toyota Prius II without any rope; the chair dangling precariously the three blocks over to her building.

Wes, the director of the city's largest theatre, lived a few blocks over. He'd arrived with wine, cheese and a movie.

"*Burlesque*, so we can talk about what a fucking delicious train wreck Cher is," he declared. "So what's new with your man, hussy?" Wes asked, opening the wine bottle.

Maggie narrowed her eyes at her best friend, Wes, who lounged across from her on a teal deco sofa. He was fifty, gorgeous, and delightfully, flamboyantly gay. The day she had started volunteering at the theatre, Maggie immediately fell in non-sexual love with Wes, and the feeling was mutual.

"He's fine," smiled Maggie.

"What do you mean 'fine'? Someone's not bringing home the hot beef injections the way they used to, or what?" Wes sipped, rolling his eyes dramatically. He served them each a glass of wine.

"Ted is, um, bringing home the bacon the very best same way he has for some time, Wes," laughed Maggie. "How many details do you want about that?"

Wes seemed to ponder for a moment.

"Hmmmm, well, he's a total hottie, but even though he's a musician, he's not vibing ANY gay, so I guess I might as well not torture myself by having to hear about his package and its delivery."

Maggie laughed again. "Well I'll spare you all the gory

details, then!"

Wes thought to himself: *Maggie looks great in this light. In her natural setting.* Her apartment over the shop was the perfect size, with its huge bay window, and stained glass panes. Her orange chair and a small painted wooden side table formed her sitting area inside the window. Large plants were everywhere. He glanced at her old MacBook, the adorable small vintage lamp, and a framed photo of her girls when they were younger, watching a town parade from the sidewalk and grinning from ear to ear.

"So, are there more wedding bells in your future? You've been dating him for*ever!*"

"Are you kidding me? I've already put one husband into a divorce court and another one's on the way in there, Wes," replied Maggie. "Why on earth would I want to put the *Marry Mag* curse on poor Ted? He hasn't done anything to deserve it."

"God, that's true," said Wes. "But I gotta say it cracks me up that you're acting like a goddamn teenager about the whole thing." He made a fake gagging motion, adding, "It's *so* cliché. I mean, seriously, when do you think he'll ask you to the prom?"

They laughed.

"I'm already shopping for my prom gown," said Maggie. "Now hand me that cheese tray."

"So how's your little whore club coming along?" asked Wes.

"We don't call it a whore club," said Maggie, raising an eyebrow. "That's an offensive term and besides, we're not getting paid. Our Scarlet Letter *Society* is simply for women who are- well, to put it in some kind of bizarre politically correct term, I guess, who are *fidelity challenged*."

"Mmhmm, *whores*. Well at least they aren't still stoning you or burning your asses at the stake anymore," said Wes, passing the Havarti and rice crackers. "The funny part is, you're in a club you technically can't even be a member of because you're not even cheating on your pretty little boyfriend! Unless you count the fact that your divorce isn't even final, which hardly counts."

"So technically, I'm still married," responded Maggie, "and thus a practicing adulteress, if you ask the Catholic Church." Making the sign of the cross while rolling her eyes, Maggie added, "And since I'm cheating on both of my husbands with Ted, I'd say I'm not just the founder of the Scarlet Letter Society, but also a quite active member."

"Well, Sister Margaret Katherine. 'Veteran Vixen Vaginas' would be a great name for your website," said Wes. "You should totally lock down a Twitter handle for that."

"We're starting to read a book each month for the Scarlet Letter Society meetings," said Maggie. "Historical or modern fiction about women who cheat on their husbands. I mean, the novels are usually written by men and end up with dead women, but it will be interesting to get the perspective on how things have changed. Or haven't. We're beginning by reading *The Scarlet Letter*."

"Ooooh! It will be like the *HO*-prah Book Club!" squealed Wes, clapping his hands.

"Let's watch the movie, goofball," Maggie said warmly.

SUBDIVISION STREETLIGHTS cast the only light through the bedroom curtains as Lisa snuck out of bed to check her email. As the floorboards creaked in a house that was only built three years before in this McNeighborhood she loathed beyond words, she knew Jim would hear her.

"Where are you going?" slurred Jim gruffly. "Don't you remember I'm going to be going away for a few days to the conference?" he asked, pulling her back into bed.

Lisa grimaced slightly.

"I was just going to get some shop paperwork done before I go into town."

So much for Jim leaving for his trip before she woke up. And here came the scene she had been hoping to avoid.

"I guess there's no time for a foot rub then," said Jim in the whiny voice that made Lisa want to drive icepicks through her own skull. She looked over at him in the bed, and then she saw it. A bright red Christian Louboutin stiletto peeked out from under his pillow.

"Jim! Those are $6000 shoes!" said Lisa, exasperated. "Why are you crushing one of them under your pillow?"

"I bought them for you, Lisa," responded Jim, sulking.

"You know I got them online for way less than that, and it's not my fault you continually refuse to indulge my fantasy."

Lisa shuddered. A foot fetish, of all things. How had she managed to marry someone with such an annoying addiction? She would never wear those stupid shoes. They weren't even new. *Gah!* Who knew where they'd been, or what she'd have to clean off them.

She thought to herself, *I have already honestly tried to go along with the whole "fantasy" thing,* as he called it. *Remember when I wore the thigh high black leather boots (and nothing else) to bed? Or how about the time I let you masturbate into a gold pair of stripper heels bought especially for the purpose?* But she was sick of him being more interested in her feet and her footwear than her preferred parts.

"Honey," she said, "I need to get to the bakery. Maybe you could just pack the shoes in your suitcase for the trip."

"Don't be mad that I spent the money. They're beautiful! Like you," said Jim.

"You damn well know we need that money for the fertility treatments," said Lisa. "I don't even want to look at them!"

She went downstairs, grabbed her laptop, and headed to the downtown bakery. *Beautiful, my ass,* she thought.

"Welcome to Keytown!" the town's sign cheerily welcomed her, and she breathed a sigh of relief. Bakery therapy. She arrived at her shop, prepared batter, popped the first batch of cinnamon buns into the oven, and washed her hands, absentmindedly wiping them to dry on her apron. She sat down at the counter stool, opened her laptop and hit "compose."

from: **Lisa** lswain@blackbirdspie.com
to: **Ben** bnidale@starfishdesign.com

date: Tuesday, May 2, 2012 at 8:10 AM
subject: My logo

Ben,
It's hard to believe we have met three times and I still don't have a mockup of my new logo. I demand customer service.
Sincerely,
Lisa Swain

She smiled as she hit 'send.' And her friends thought she was licking cherry juice off this guy? Geez, wouldn't that be amazing. So far in real life versus Scarlet Letter Club fantasy league, she'd simply had two "brainstorming" lunches and a shop visit to "gather information." And of course the email fluttering back and forth like middle school notes passed from classmate to classmate. *Is Ben taking a long time to produce my business materials so he can prolong this?* Lisa thought, doubting herself. *Or am I just being silly? He's probably just busy.*

Ping, came the sound of a new email, and her heart rate

quickened.

> from: **Ben** <u>bnidale@starfishdesign.com</u>
> to: **Lisa** lswain@blackbirdspie.com
>
> date: Tuesday, May 2, 2012, 8:13 AM
> subject: Your pie
>
>> You know that I feel strongly about the image that is presented for your business, and that I'm trying to get a feel for the message you want to send to your customers. Don't try to rush the creative process.
>>
>> Are you free for lunch? We can discuss this further, as customer satisfaction is my goal.
>
> Ben

The blush crept up from her neckline to her face as Lisa nervously wiped her hands off again on her apron before hitting "reply."

> from: **Lisa** <u>lswain@blackbirdspie.com</u>
> to: **Ben** bnidale@starfishdesign.com
>
> date: Tuesday, May 2, 2012 at 8:17 AM

subject: Customer satisfaction

> Thank you for your prompt response. I
> agree a lunch meeting is in order. Meet
> me at Provence at noon.

> L

Oh yeah, middle school was definitely on the phone, wanting their geeky note-passing routine back. What was it about written communication that made it so sexy? Lisa stood up, realizing she had just sent out a lunch invitation. She looked at the clock, and down at her beat-up Gap jeans and worn cotton t-shirt. *I can't wear this to the Provence.* A visit to Maggie's shop for something to wear was in order as soon as those cinnamon buns came out of the oven.

ZARINA SMILED as the women entered the shop for their monthly meeting.

"Good morning, Zarina," said Maggie as she came in. "Always good to start the day at Z's!"

Zarina's mom had never really 'decorated' the shop per se, just covered it in a scattering of 80s memorabilia she'd picked up over the years at yard sales and online auctions. Pac Man memorabilia, Bon Jovi posters, shadow boxes of scratch-and-sniff sticker and Garbage Pail Kids cards, plastic

Gremlins, and other vintage trinkets bedecked the shop. On the wall hung a large 80s-font print featuring a shop-namesake quote: "Screws fall out all the time; the world's an imperfect place."

Eva and Lisa crossed to the brown leather couch area as Zarina locked the door behind the ladies. She didn't flip over the 'open' sign since their monthly meeting was private and the shop didn't technically open for another hour. She busied herself getting their standard order ready: two Neo Maxi double espressos, a caramel macchiato for the bakery lady, Lisa, plus warming up the blueberry muffins she baked last night.

"So how's everything with Ben, Lisa? And have you figured out a way to deal with that foot fetish husband of yours?" Eva smiled.

"Ben and I took a walk the other day to Bailey Park," said Lisa, "and we ended up having sex in broad daylight under the covered bridge."

Maggie and Eva laughed. "Well that's a new one," said Maggie. "Bravo, kid. You're lucky Keytown's finest weren't patrolling the park at the time—or worse, some poor mom and a toddler going for a walk."

Lisa grinned, cursing herself for making up such an outrageous story.

"Well I got a can of homemade whipped cream unleashed into my vag," said Eva, breaking into laughter. "The chef had prepared it especially to be organic."

"That was thoughtful," said Maggie. "I mean, you wouldn't want any of that trashy-ass grocery store canned whipped cream up there."

"It was of course delicious, too, when I sprayed some on him and got to taste it during the expert blow job I served up."

Lisa, ever the junior member of the club, asked, "Where did you learn to give great blowjobs? I mean, I've been married for five years and dated before that, and of course there's Ben now, but I've always worried I'm not good at it. Not to mention I don't like it. I did order the spray we talked about last month..."

"Art of the Blowjob," said Maggie and Eva at the same time, chuckling.

"What's that?" asked Lisa, fishing her journal out of her purse.

Maggie replied, "It's a website where this auburn haired chick does instructional videos on how to give the perfect blowjob. It's not porny or tacky. It's quite helpful!"

Eva added, "You have to admit it is kind of hilarious that there is just this, like, DICK that appears from the left side of the screen. You never ever even see the guy."

"He must be a pretty happy guy," said Lisa.

"Yeah, nice work if you can get it, huh?" said Maggie.

Eva took a sip of her coffee. "So what's the latest in your ever-active love life, Mags?"

"Divorce number two will be final pretty soon. Everything

is going fine with Ted, but I actually have a new friend now, too."

"Holy Mary Magdelene loving Jesus!" declared Eva. "Can you ever just be shagging one person, Margaret Hanson?"

"Well if that ain't the tramp kettle calling the slut pot black, I don't know what is," snorted Maggie as a grin spread across her face, now lined with smile lines at 47. She crossed her vintage cowboy boots and adjusted her brown corduroy skirt.

"It so happens," announced Maggie, "that I'm sort of cheating on my lover with a very adorable professional in town."

"A professional what?" laughed Eva with an eye roll. "So what's this one's name?"

"Well, smarty pants," said Maggie, "I'll have to tell you all about it later."

As the women left the shop, Zarina raised the store's front window shade and flipped the sign to "open." Then she texted her boyfriend, Stanley. He loved to come over and hear all about the morning meeting, especially since it always made her a little horny for some reason. Flying estrogen? She entered two words into her battered iPhone 3: "Booty. Call."

When Maggie asked if Zarina could have two copies of *The Scarlet Letter* (Eva read on a Kindle app), she was happy to accommodate her favorite customers, and appreciated them supporting the store. She found three gently used copies at a great price, ordering the extra copy for herself. Ha! *I will be in their book club and they won't even know it*, she thought, laughing to herself.

Zarina smiled at Stanley as he entered the shop a short time later.

"Yes, I'm here for one Booty Latte, extra cream, please," he smiled.

"Coming right up," said Zarina, winking at him.

I love how much fun we have together, thought Zarina as she made his coffee, *and how he makes me laugh.*

Stanley interrupted her coffee making by grabbing her from behind and planting heated kisses on her neck. She turned, put down the cup, and pulled him by the belt hook of his jeans into the small bathroom. She locked the door. Just the necessary amounts of clothes peeled away as he scooped her up onto the bathroom sink. *Nothing like forbidden sex*, thought Zarina, smiling at the possibility of a customer coming into the store at any time.

Ten minutes later, Stanley and Zarina were sitting on the couch next to each other, playing Words with Friends together on their phones.

Stanley looked at Zarina.

"Thanks for being my old person," he said, and gave that silly, crooked grin that simply undid her.

When Stanley came into her shop for coffee one day, they just sort of clicked: finishing each other's sentences, laughing at stupid things no one else would think were funny. Stanley joked that they were kind of like… old people who would play on a Scrabble board in their retirement community in the same way they played WWF on iPhones. *It's the same game, seriously,* he'd said.

"I love being old people with you," she said.

Love is awesome, thought Zarina. *Except when it sucks.* She listened to the ladies at the SLS club each month, and they talk about doomed love and who's having sex with whom. *I mean Jesus Christ,* she'd tell Stanley, *these bitches are horny!*

"Maybe they're in some kind of full blown mid-life crisis," Stanley had said, *"but man, they do seem to be gettin' it on."*

Zarina believed, despite it sounding "all hippy-dippy" as her mom would say… she believed *love* is the thing, not sex. It was about the *personal relationship;* the intimacy of spirits, not bodies. You can have sex with anybody. Love only happens with someone really, really special.

She put down the Words With Friends game she was currently winning and brewed some coffee. It made the world go round, and all.

Her day's first customer checked out and left, and the sound of the door clicking behind her threw Maggie into a trance.

The dreaded sound: a soft click of the front door locked behind her mother as she left. 9-1-1 was written in huge letters next to the phone. Maggie always pretended to be asleep so her mother wouldn't worry she'd been awake and frightened. Maggie would watch the minutes tick by on the old-fashioned alarm clock, and sometimes it would be 2:35 or 3:07. And then one day, her mother packed Maggie's things into two brown paper grocery store bags and brought her to the home of a foster family. She told her she loved her, that she didn't want her to feel cold or be in the dark anymore, and then she was gone. Maggie was six. She never saw her mother again.

The gentle tinkling of the small bell that hung from the handle of the 1884 original door to her Victorian commercial building once again served as an alarm to Maggie's daymare. She grabbed a pill from her purse and chased it with a sip of her coffee. Putting down her copy of *The Scarlet Letter*, she saw Ted as he entered the shop. He was holding a handful of peonies. When she saw the flowers, she knew two things: that they'd come from the huge light pink bush near his building across town, and that he'd already taken them inside to wash off all the ants that perpetually plagued the sweet-smelling blooms.

"Good morning, beautiful lady," he said, dramatically presenting her with the handful of freshly cut (and only slightly drippy) blooms.

Maggie smiled like a schoolgirl. She loved the way he always said "good morning" to her, even if it wasn't morning. She thanked him, took the flowers and put them in a big, old turquoise Ball jar on the counter.

"Thank you for that ant removal service, dahlin," she

said, and Ted grinned at her pronunciation: her New England accent had always been sexy to him. "It was nice of you to remember I love peonies, but hate ants."

When she finished with the flowers, she walked around the counter and put her arms around his neck. He returned her kiss eagerly with a soft, exploratory prod of the tongue followed by a gentle grazing of her upper lip with his teeth. She slapped him playfully on the butt of his worn, faded jeans.

"You know, I'm open for business around here, mistah, and it's not that kind of business."

"I'd like to have you open for business right now upstairs, ma'am," said Ted. He grabbed the curly auburn ponytail through the hole in the back of her baseball hat, looked into her green eyes, and pulled the cap of her hat aside so he could kiss her.

Maggie found herself glancing over at the clock. 10:30. *Hmmm.* It was a slower time of morning, but she didn't know if she could risk someone coming into the shop, especially close to lunchtime. She narrowed her eyes at him. He looked back at her, his tall frame in a fake slump, his hazel eyes drooping, and a ridiculous cartoonish frown on his face. It was the glance down at those faded jeans that won her over, for it was there that she saw his very enthusiastic interest in her. His passion for her never seemed to end, and she sighed.

Looking directly at his rising erection, she said, "You win. The customer is always right."

She walked over, quickly locked the door to the shop, and hastily hung the "Back in 30 Minutes" sign on the door.

She took off her red vintage 1980s Snoopy half-apron as she walked toward the back narrow staircase to the upstairs apartment. She looked over her shoulder and smiled at his fake running motion and wide eyes.

She stopped on the fifth step up.

"I don't think I can make it all the way up to my apartment," she smiled sheepishly.

"No need," said Ted.

He stopped on the third step and grabbed her around her waist. He lifted the vintage Sesame Street t-shirt and kissed her belly. She raked her hands through his curly mop of dark hair and kissed him with all the desire she'd felt from the moment he'd entered the shop. They never seemed to be able to get enough of each other.

She eagerly dashed her tongue into his mouth, moaning when he returned the kiss with equal excitement. She leaned back on the wooden step and lifted her hips to feel the full effect of his complete hardness.

Grinding her jeans against his, they both sighed in anticipation of their typically amazing lovemaking.

Ted lifted her t-shirt over her head, her Boston Red Sox baseball cap falling onto the step as her moppy curls spilled out. She tugged at the button fly of his jeans as he removed her bra in a matter of seconds. Then his mouth was on her nipples, and once again she rested back on the step. His tongue, his teeth, the pressure—everything was perfect and she found herself grinding on his hard-on until her body exploded. She shook as he started to undo her jeans.

He smiled down at her as he gently twisted her nipples with his expert thumbs and forefingers. She managed to gather herself, her shirt, her bra, her hat, and turn to go up the stairs.

"We would probably be more comfortable upstairs," said Maggie, clearing her throat and still shaky from the intense orgasm. *Dry humping! At my age!* She smiled at Ted.

"I kinda like these steps," he said, following her and grabbing her hips. Still both in jeans, he pressed his hardness against the crease between her back pockets. She lowered her jeans over her hips so she could feel every bit of that stiffness, automatically leaning into a sort of modified downward-facing dog yoga pose. She wore no panties under her jeans. Happy for the access, he reached around to her front and slipped two fingers into her, sliding them effortlessly in and out as he circled his hips around her ass.

Maggie enjoyed this amazing sensation for a few moments, and then couldn't take it anymore—it was time for his jeans to go.

She reached behind her and lowered his already-unbuttoned jeans. She felt him step out of them and his boxers and now, finally, she could feel him against her. She reached back to stroke him and he moaned softly in appreciation. She flipped back over, sitting on her jeans to cushion her from the hardwood floor steps.

She felt him move down two steps, scoop his arms under her waist to raise her toward his mouth, and he used his tongue to arouse her even more, if that was possible. She rested her head on her arm and let herself get close to another orgasm, but this time, she wanted him inside her. She reached down, grabbing his toned waist, and lifted him up toward her, gently stroking him for a few moments before bringing him closer to her. She teased him there for a moment until he couldn't take it anymore and entered her with every inch of himself.

They both made the same sound-- a release of tension, sexual energy, passion, complete bliss. He began to move inside her and she arched her back to meet his thrusts. They expertly worked against each other, pleasure cascading into simultaneous orgasms.

They sighed, then laughed. He followed her up to the apartment so they could grab a quick shower before moving on with their days.

Maggie chatted with Ted in the shop for a few minutes before he had to get back to work.

"I had an interesting experience last week," she said, wondering if this was really a good time to be talking about it.

"Oh yeah, what's that?" Ted smiled.

"I met someone new. A professor at the college."

"Don't tell me you're cheating on both your estranged

soon-to-be-ex-husband and me with some hot chemistry professor hunk," he said, teasingly.

"Actually, no, it's not a chemistry professor," said Maggie, feeling slightly awkward about how this conversation was going to go. "It's a literature professor, a customer here at the shop."

Ted looked quizzically at her.

"So what, he's a new boy toy, someone you want to have a threesome with that includes me, or what?"

Maggie looked at Ted. They had an open, honest relationship and she knew that the news would not be something he would be completely shocked by. He was pretty sexually liberal. Divorced, he had dated a number of women, encountering during his work as a musician some non-vanilla stuff, including a few threesomes she was aware of.

"Just a hook-up, I guess," she said, although she looked uncertain about it.

Ted laughed. A deep, hearty laugh from all the way down in his stomach. She glanced admiringly at the wrinkles the smile created on his face. The gray hairs sprinkled in with the dark brown were so sexy, she thought as he ran his fingers through it.

"Maggie, you sex queen, you!"

"I'm certainly not a sex queen," Maggie responded. "This must just be some kind of fluke thing. I mean, I was attracted to the professor, and we sort of hooked up, and I don't know what it means or what is happening."

Ted walked over, pushing the freshly re-fitted baseball cap aside again, and kissed her passionately. But as he pulled away he had a huge grin as he asked, "Is this the part where we start using the term 'mid-life crisis?' Are the professor and I here because you need us to make you feel young again?"

Maggie smiled at Ted and straightened her baseball cap.

"I don't know what to call it," said Maggie.

The shop entry bell jingled again.

"Hey Lisa!" said Maggie as her friend walked in. Ted beamed from ear to ear watching Maggie blush. He knew her glance at the clock meant she was thankful Lisa hadn't arrived ten minutes earlier.

"Hi Ted," said Lisa. "Good morning, Maggie. I have an, um, a sudden lunch meeting and I came downtown today in these ratty clothes. I was wondering if you could help me find something to wear."

"Of course, dear," she responded, and Lisa loved the way it sounded: *de-ah.*

Ted hugged Maggie goodbye, and she thanked him again for the flowers.

Maggie looked at Lisa. "We're going to want to find an outfit that says, *I'm just the local baker, but please fuck me under the covered bridge again,* then?"

June 2012

"I know where you goin' to, I knew when you came home
last night
'Cause your eyes had a mist from the smoke of a distant
fire."
— "Smoke From a Distant Fire," Sanford Townsend Band

Monthly meeting of the Scarlet Letter Society.
Zoomdweebies Café
Friday, June 1, 2012
5:30 a.m.

"Welcome to Z's, ladies," said Zarina, opening the shop to the beautiful June morning and its fresh sunrise.

"Hey there, Zarina," said Eva. "You look awfully bright and chipper this early morning."

She smiled.

"This must have something to do with that slightly brooding but completely adorable young hipster gentleman we often see visiting your lovely shop," added Eva.

"Well, I hadn't thought about it that way," replied Zarina, "but I guess that's just a good a reason as any to put a smile on my face. And you know we hate being called hipsters."

"We know," said Maggie. "But what else are we supposed to call you youngins? And by the way, thanks for getting the books for us this month, hipster."

"No problem, Mag Hag. You don't mind if I call you that, right? Only every time you call me a hipster." Zarina winked at Maggie, enjoying her fake horror face response, and retreated behind the counter to begin supplying the early morning caffeine.

Maggie began the meeting with her typical style. "Ok, so which of you adultresses read the book? You know, the one our entire tiny club is named after?"

Lisa cleared her throat. "I read it. It's not an easy thing to do. That old-fashioned language made me remember why we all read Cliffs Notes back in the day. But the theme of sin and the conflict between heart and mind are timeless."

"Well that was a thought-provoking, brief but detailed book review, Lisa. Thank you for that," said Maggie. Eva laughed.

"What are you laughing about, missy? I bet your big-shot corporate-attorney ass didn't even read page one," said Maggie.

"I did so read page one!" proclaimed Eva. "Plus more than half of the Wikipedia page." They laughed.

Lisa always found herself a little jealous of the relationship between Maggie and Eva, who'd known each other for years. Lisa hated feeling like the perpetual third wheel on the SLS bike, but the current company represented her only friends, so she did her best to swallow her insecurity.

"The whole first page of the book, huh? Wow, we're impressed," said Maggie. "Well, ladies, how about if I give my thoughts on the book? I actually took notes."

"Notes? Geez!" said Eva.

"I took notes, too," admitted Lisa, clutching her trusty notebook and flipping through it.

"Pipe down, Eva. It looks like our little book club discussion is being led by me and Lisa, since you barely cracked the cover—er, opened the app," said Maggie. She continued, "There's a reason all of our club invites include the one quote about the scarlet letter as 'her passport into regions where other women dared not tread.' I picked it because it describes that there are basically two types of women in this world. Those who cheat, and those who do not."

Lisa looked down at her coffee, then pretended to write something down in her journal.

"Well I guess we've come to the right place," said Eva. "I know I'd rather be the mistress than the wife."

Lisa turned to Eva and said, "But you are a wife."

Eva replied, "I didn't say I wasn't, but in addition to the fact that I'm a terrible one, obviously, I think being a mistress is so much more fun. There's no laundry or kids' sports practices or fights about spending money. It's just fun."

"Which brings up another key quote from the book: 'She had not known the weight until she felt the freedom'," said Maggie. "I think that's what Hawthorne was trying to say there. Being in a marriage can feel like you have the weight of the world on your shoulders. But when you're with a lover, you're in another world, and you're free. Even if it means you pay the price of a sinner."

"Exactly," said Eva. "Sin or no sin, it's an escape from reality. And if you're with several lovers, you're even more free! Right, Maggie?"

Maggie sighed. "Why do I have the feeling that we're never going to end up actually discussing the books in our book club? Ok, well, since you seem to be asking, Eva, the professor and I are just friends."

"Margaret Katherine Hanson, I believe you just blushed for the first time in the history of your half-century life," said Eva.

"Fuck you, half-century!" said Maggie. "I'm nowhere near fifty yet!"

Lisa looked at the two women and laughed nervously, secretly worrying she didn't fit in to this club. She scribbled in her journal and thought to herself: *how am I going to keep coming to these meetings if I'm contributing literally only fictionalized accounts of fantasy encounters with my graphic designer? I love Maggie and Eva's stories and their confidence, but will it be enough for me to take the leap and have a real affair of my own?*

Zarina listened intently to the June meeting of the Scarlet Letter Society and wondered to herself who Maggie's new professor friend was; whether it was a friend of her mother's at the college. She observed the group dynamic of the women. Maggie was clearly the leader. The confidence in her boisterous New England accent alone could have made a ship full of men sail toward a hurricane if that's what they'd been told to do.

Eva was more serious generally and seemed so conflicted. One time she'd seem happy, giddy almost, and another day she'd seem kind of moody and somber. And Lisa? Well, she just seemed to be in a world all her own. She often came into the shop and wrote quietly; alone. She was so much more reserved than the other women. Her quiet nature always made Zarina wonder how she even got the nerve to have an affair.

But when Zarina heard the women talking about another book selection, she couldn't help but chime in. *Anna Karenina?* Ugh. Zarina had an immediate sneaking suspicion the women would not enjoy trudging through the 1852 Tolstoy classic. She'd read it herself in her last semester at college. At the meeting, Maggie had come in with the *Anna*

Karenina opening quote,

"*Happy families are all alike; every unhappy family is unhappy in its own way.*"

It was true the women often talked about their own families—who had lost a parent (Lisa), whose mother was getting a bit senile (Eva), and who was orphaned as a kid (Maggie, who spent a fortune in therapy trying to get over those years that were so difficult to forget). But Zarina knew the book would end up being torture, if any of them even got through the tome. So she approached Maggie.

"I hate to interrupt," said Zarina. "And of course I'm happy to order you ladies any book you want. But I'm not sure any of you will like reading this one." Zarina understood their desire to find wisdom and meaning in adulterous literature. But there was no sense letting them read voluminous Tolstoy about a woman treated as a social outcast...especially since Anna committed suicide at the end by hurling herself in front of a damn train.

"What about *Fear of Flying* by Erica Jong?" asked Zarina. She knew Maggie's shop was named for the 70s novel, as was her daughter Erica, who Zarina had gone to school with as a kid.

"Oh, for the love of baby Jesus," Maggie had said, laughing. "How have we not read it already?" She told Zarina to order copies just before they left.

She was looking forward to reading it. Her mom had spoken fondly of the "feminist bible," and she was eager to see what Jong's take on the whole infidelity thing would be.

IT WAS barely 7 am as Eva sat in her eighth floor office building near Union Station in Washington, D.C. She thought about her boys. After a week of being "unplugged", she thought the boys had learned their lesson and hopefully wouldn't get busted doing stupid shit again.

Disciplining the boys had triggered her memory of the kinds of discipline that were doled out in her home as a kid. Her dad would drink, get drunk, scream at her mother for some ridiculous housewife violation—the laundry was piled up, why was the dishwasher not emptied, why couldn't she *just vacuum this fucking room?* And then, on the bad days, he would hit her. Eva would hide in her bedroom closet until it was over.

Stay out of his way, just stay out of his way. When the attacks came, whether verbal or physical, Eva's mother would look down shamefully, never yelling back, never fighting. She just took it. To this day, living alone on the island, her abusive drunk asshole of a husband long dead, she was as vacant as an abandoned motel. It was like life had battered her down into a state of complacency that amounted to just waiting to die.

Eva found herself getting lost in her thoughts a lot. It was difficult to concentrate at work when she had so much going on in her personal life. The paperwork stacked on the desk in front of her demanded her attention for the big trial coming up. She wanted to prepare for it, but thoughts of her troubled marriage, wayward sons, New York chef lover, and her intern Ron, were constantly getting in her way.

The monthly visits to Maryland's Eastern Shore were the only time she really had to herself to try to put her life into some kind of perspective. Her mother's cottage on Matthew's Island had a separate small caretaker's cottage where Eva stayed when she visited. Her mom had become more and more forgetful as time went on, and once a month was the minimum Eva could visit in order to make sure her mother was getting along okay.

"Going to your happy place?" asked Ron as he peeked his blond head around the corner into her office door.

Ron walked in, observing Eva staring at the enormous vintage apothecary jar on the corner of her desk. It was filled with sea glass she found on the island. It was a hobby she'd picked up from her mom. Searching for the worn pieces of glass tossed onto the beach by the Chesapeake Bay was her personal form of relaxation—

therapy even. She'd check the low tide charts, then ride a bike over to the hidden spot she'd found where the best variety of colors could be found. The most typical colors: white, brown, and green were found in abundance but the jar before her held only the pale turquoise she loved best. Though she had jars filled with other colors at the cottage, her office collection represented her favorite color, each piece collected at a moment of peace not otherwise found in her life.

Eva smiled at Ron. He was gorgeous in his sleek black suit, perfect grin, huge blue eyes staring at her eagerly.

"That sounds like a fantastic idea," she said.

Ron walked over and closed the door.

"You know, you never invite me on your New York trips," he said, smiling at Eva. "I'd love to get out of DC once in a while."

"Yeah, sometime we'll have to do that," said Eva, immediately thinking that she'd have to find a reason to stay in a different hotel, because there was no way in hell she could stay at her usual Plaza suite and have the worlds of her two very different lovers collide. "But for now, why don't we get out of here and take a coffee break?"

"And by coffee break, I am guessing you mean at my apartment?" Ron beamed at her, acting surprised at the invitation.

She grabbed her purse and they left the office separately, walking the few blocks to his apartment building.

"What's the matter today?" asked Ron as they walked up the steps and into his loft space apartment in an old warehouse building. "You look a world away." Eva sat on a tan leather chair, plopping her feet on its ottoman as Ron fixed cups of coffee for both of them. She asked for Bailey's in hers. When he returned from the small kitchen, she saw that he had unbuttoned his yellow Oxford shirt, smiling as he walked over to her with the steaming cup.

"Oh, it's nothing, just thinking about my day," said Eva. "Which looks like it might be getting better already."

Ron's black pants hung low on his hips. His blond hair was tousled, and Eva admired his perfect chest and abs as he put the coffee down on the table next to where she was seated. She took two long swallows of the coffee, not minding the heat burning down through her chest. *What is that thing called*, Eva wondered, as she ran her hand over that smooth area of skin just inside Ron's hip bones, that amazing V-shaped valley thing? Whatever its name, there wasn't a doubt it was singlehandedly responsible for the wrecking of homes and the falls of empires.

"Well, let's start your day off right," said Ron as he leaned down in front of her seat. Since they had texted about a "coffee break" just this morning, he knew she wouldn't have wasted time wearing panties underneath her short gray designer skirt. Panties would be in her Coach bag, nice and clean for the office later.

Eva removed her blouse and placed it neatly over a nearby chair. She wore only a cream lace bra and the skirt. She picked up the mug of coffee and sipped it again, knowing it was about to get cold. She smiled at her young lover.

"Whenever I see you before work, I know it's going to be a good day," said Eva. Ron hiked up her skirt. She lifted her hips and sat on the back of the overstuffed chair. She unfastened the zipper of her skirt as he gently kissed the insides of her thighs. She mentally high-fived herself for remembering to shave the tops of her legs.

Ron's hands were strong but gentle. He ran them up the sides of her legs, across the sides of her tiny waist, and slowly up that magical spot next to her breasts. She shivered, goosebumps rising on her thin frame, her nipples growing hard. She moaned quietly, willing his hands to graze across her breasts. As he kneeled on the chair in front of her, she deftly used her feet to acknowledge his growing erection.

He smiled and as he stood up to disrobe, Eva admired his body once again. She slid down the back of the chair so she was seated in front of his obvious arousal. They had only been lovers for a few months; she'd interviewed him for the position he'd take after he completed law school, which was just last month. But by now, she knew his body well. She took him into her hands, and using what she considered a fine skill set, she began licking and teasing him until he was both moaning and fully excited. He throbbed with desire, and she loved feeling that in her mouth. Quietly cursing her gag reflex, she used the spray she'd grabbed from her purse to spritz the back of her throat. She gently but firmly grasped him, using her lips to stimulate him. Her other hand grabbed his amazing ass. She felt his knees get weak as she continued, stopping before he got too close to orgasm.

Then suddenly he used his strong arms to cup her body and scoop her off the chair. Ron carried her into the bedroom and tossed her on the bed playfully. He grabbed her thighs and pulled her to the edge of the bed. He knelt, now kissing the insides of her thighs with more urgency.

Eva was never good at accepting oral sex. She felt guilty she wasn't doing anything to stimulate the guy, had difficulty relaxing enough to enjoy it, and found it really took too long for her to come this way, adding more guilt. She cursed her inner guilty Catholic, trying to relax and enjoy.

Then she had an idea. The bed had sturdy wooden sides. She was in fantastic shape from practicing yoga three times a week, so she slid her body down toward the kneeling (and somewhat surprised-looking) Ron. Using her strong arms, she held her weight up on the wooden side rail and slid over him. The squat position gave her complete control, and she rose up and down, gliding her hips in a circular fashion that made both Ron and Eva moan with pleasure.

Finally, back in control.

MAGGIE AND Wes sat down at their window table overlooking Fritchie Creek on the lovely early summer day in Keytown. Bento boxes at Café Tokyo were their favorite lunch.

"So how are things going with your man?" asked Maggie.

"I can't believe I broke my own law and dated an actor," said Wes with a sigh. "As a theatre director, I know better than anyone that they're all whores and emotional disaster zones."

"But he's hot," said Maggie.

"Alfred is so fucking hot that when he walks down the theatre aisle toward the stage, I literally get goosebumps. And I swear to God, having a hot affair inside an empty theatre is the sexiest thing ever. We're all kinds of *Gay Phantom of the Opera* up in this house. H-O-T."

Maggie laughed, "Hilarious. Could the two of you please stereotype yourselves a little bit more? You're like gay cliché central!"

"I know, right?" said Wes. "And don't care. He is a stunner, and I swear to God, a keeper. This is the longest I've dated anyone—ever. Six months! The whole thing is positively mythical."

"I am so, so happy for you," said Maggie. She'd never seen Wes so serious about a guy, and she didn't want to jinx how happy he was by talking too much about it. She secretly hoped this was the one for Wes—like herself, at the end of the day, he just wanted someone to curl up and watch bad movies and drink good booze with.

The pair ordered their bento boxes and hot teas and took in the scenery of the passersby on the waterfront. They both loved people-watching.

"I'm getting too old for this shit," said Maggie.

"What shit, baby?" asked Wes.

"My hip joints were killing me for days after my little stairwell romp with Ted," she said. "And starting another fling is making me wonder what the hell is going on with me."

"Oooooh, yeah, what's the latest with you and Dr. Feelgood?"

"I haven't told anyone but you that the professor is a woman! We've seen each other a few times. I really like her. I positively get the whole girl thing now; it's a totally different world sexually. I mean, I don't think I'm a lesbian, because at the end of the day, seriously, just give me a dick."

"Word!" said Wes.

"It's almost like finding a new best girlfriend that you're just more intimate with," said Maggie. "I have generally never felt very close to other women. I hate cliques and all that, so the idea of having a single best girlfriend is something I've always wished I had. Kate is filling a void that I guess I've always had and didn't even realize."

"Sounds like you sure are getting your void filled, honey. And awww. How cute are you girls? Painting each other's toenails, watching *Heathers* together, and sucking each other's tits."

Maggie sighed. "It's not like that, exactly. Although I do have to say after a lifetime of wondering what it would be like to be with a girl, I can say it's much easier than I imagined. Everything just happens sorta naturally. Girls are softer. Their hair is so soft! Everyone must use better conditioner than I do. And the curves...wow. It's far different than a guy."

"Oh I'm sure, not that I'd know about the whole girl thing," said Wes. "I practically gagged in 7th grade when we played spin the bottle and I had to make out with this cheerleader. All I could think about was that I wanted to play on the turns where it was only guys in the circle. It was her football player boyfriend I wanted to make out with! So, have you told Ted about the good doctor?"

"Sort of," said Maggie. "Wasn't sure if I should tell Dave about it."

"Husband number one! Say what? What is the deal with you two, anyway? How do you still manage to be friends with him after all the marriages the two of you have been through?" asked Wes.

"There haven't been that many marriages," said Maggie. "I'm only just divorcing my second husband, and Dave divorced that idiot girl he married after me within eighteen months."

"So what's the deal with Ted, then, since you said you don't have any plans to marry him?" Wes asked.

"Aw, he's just a filler," said Maggie.

"And what the fuck is a filler?" asked Wes.

"You know, just like when you have a guy to keep your mind off the fact that you don't have *the guy*," said Maggie. "When I realized how miserable I was with Matt and that I wanted a divorce, Ted was just sort of there to be a lovely distraction. He's sweet, and fun and low maintenance."

"And hot! I guess I was wrong thinking you might be in love with this guy," said Wes. "And I certainly understand being in a place where you have a guy to keep your mind off not having *the* guy. Don't miss that."

Maggie thought for a second. "Who the fuck knows about any of it," she said. "I have for sure learned a lot about what love is and what it isn't over the years. There are different theories on whether you find it once or you can find it a hundred times, and I am starting to think I had my shot at love in my first marriage, blew it, and now I'm just sort of going to be doing the filler thing."

"Oh, Jesus, let's just not even go down the 'love' road," said Wes. "What a bunch of greeting card industry-fueled bullshit that is. It all comes down to who makes you feel good about yourself and pays attention to you. That's what I'm getting out of the actor right now; he makes me feel sexy. Call it love, call it lust, call it whatever. I just want more of it! And not to be sentimental about the whole thing, but when I am with him I feel like I'm home."

"Yeah," said Maggie. "I want more of something, too. I want to feel home. I'm just not there yet."

As she said headed back to her shop after lunch with Wes, Maggie's phone rang. The noise startled her, and she didn't even look to see who was calling before she answered it.

"Hello?" said Maggie.

"It's just me," said the voice on the other line.

"Well of course it's you," said Maggie, smiling. "Who else would call me on the actual phone?"

"How is everything going?"

"Well, fine, I guess. I'm about to go through a divorce

and I'm cheating on my soon-to-be ex with both a guy and a chick. So I guess I'm pretty busy. How 'bout you?"

"The same. A chick?" Dave laughed. "That's new. Old buildings still falling. Trying to keep a few of them up."

Maggie smiled. "Old buildings still falling" was the standard answer whenever anyone asked her first husband how he was doing. Dave was an architectural historian for the National Historic Preservation Association in Washington, D.C., working out of their regional Keytown office. His passion for old buildings had fueled a career that included several books, speaking gigs around the globe, and the very thing he loved most and did best: doing anything in his power to save beautiful historic buildings from being torn down.

"I know there are a few old beauties out there still on the planet thanks to you standing in front of the bulldozer," said Maggie.

"Maybe one. Okay, maybe two," said Dave. "I thought I'd give you a call to talk about Lilith's graduation party."

"Aw, I'm too tired to tell you about it," said Maggie. "But can you believe our baby is graduating already? Let's have lunch tomorrow and we can go over it all then, ok?"

"Sounds good. I'll come by your shop?"

"Sure. You know I'm always hungry by noon, so I'll see you then."

"Perfect. See you then, Maggie."

"Bye, Dave."

from: **Lisa** lswain@blackbirdspie.com
to: **Ben** bnidale@starfishdesign.com

date: Monday, June 11 2012 at 7:09 AM
subject: Logos

> Thank you again for the lovely lunch
> at the Provence. Their crepes are to
> die for — and I'm picky about crepes. I
> appreciate you sending over the logo
> samples. They look fantastic. Would
> you like to meet here at the bakery to
> discuss them?

Lisa swallowed as she hit send. Oh, geez, this was going to be it. Inviting Ben directly to the shop after the incredible sexual tension they'd shared at their lunch was a bold move; one that would make the SLS proud if they had any idea all she was doing was flirting.

How am I even thinking about cheating on Jim? she wrote in her journal. But it was right underneath the words "EYE FUCKING" in huge letters, with a cartoon eye drawing surrounded by squiggles. Other than his ridiculous foot fetish, Jim really wasn't that bad of a husband. He had been by her side when she went through heartbreak after heartbreak trying to get pregnant. She flipped through the journal pages, seeing the dates and times written down in the margin. He would drive home from work if it was ovulation time, go to doctor's appointments with her, bring dinner home when he knew she'd had a long day at work.

In the beginning of their relationship, undoubtedly when he was trying to play it down, she hadn't thought the shoes obsession had been that big of a deal. Lisa wasn't someone who had cared what the hell she wore on her feet—if it were up to her, she'd be in flip flops every day at the bakery. But she now had a custom built closet full of the most expensive, most gorgeous shoes on the planet. Carrie Bradshaw would have fainted at the sight of this obscene closet. They actually called it the "Shoe Room" because it used to be the house's smallest bedroom.

All I want is a baby, she wrote, *and all I have are shoes.*

She heard the soft *ping* of her laptop that meant a new message had arrived.

from: **Ben** bnidale@starfishdesign.com
to: **Lisa** lswain@blackbirdspie.com

date: Monday, June 11, 2012, 7:16 AM

subject: Business meetings

Perhaps needless to say, I would absolutely love to meet you at your bakery to discuss your logo. I want you to be happy. Whichever mock-ups you like, we can change until we achieve exactly what you want.

May I be so forward as to say that I really very much enjoyed our lunch as well. You looked gorgeous in the outfit from Maggie's shop. I was sorry to have to leave town for that conference and not get to follow up sooner. As always, I am looking forward to seeing you again.

Ben

Lisa smiled, wondering what would happen at the meeting. She re-opened her journal. While many times she could fill three pages without even blinking, sometimes she'd write only a word or two with the date. Today, she scrawled the date and the words, *Design THIS.*

July 2012

"We're undercover passion on the run
Chasing love up against the sun
We're strangers by day, lovers by night
Knowing it's so wrong, but feeling so right."
-"Part Time Lovers," Stevie Wonder

Monthly meeting of the Scarlet Letter Society.
Zoomdweebies Café
Friday, July 6, 2012
5:30 a.m.

Attention, ladies! We're terrible at being a book club. This month make sure you have read Erica Jong's **Fear of Flying** *(stay up all night if you have to, Eva!). It's my favorite book, so I'd love to actually chat about it.*

> "The scarlet letter was her passport into regions where other women dared not tread."
> -*The Scarlet Letter*, Nathaniel Hawthorne

At 6:00 a.m., Eva checked the email reminder of that week's book club meeting as the notification came up on her iPhone. Knowing she was going to catch crap from Maggie, she had at least read a few chapters of this one. It certainly was an easier read than that Victorian snoozer she'd blown off. At least this one took place in a period of time during which they'd all actually been alive.

Eva rolled over in the luxurious, ridiculously high Egyptian cotton thread count bedding in her two-story suite overlooking Central Park. *God*, she thought, *I love it here*. And how could she not? This top-notch suite was compliments of her hard work and dedication to her corporate law practice, and she had earned it. She rolled her eyes at the thought. *Okay, that was all kinda bullshit.* She knew full well the room upgrade was compliments of her chef lover. She used to stay in a normal person small suite, not this place, twice the size of her mother's island cottage, where actual presidents had stayed.

Her hotel phone rang. *Who used these anymore?* she thought as she answered.

A French accent greeted her on the other line. "Good morning, Madame Eva Bradley?"

"Yessssss?" she answered.

"This is Charles, the head chef here at the Plaza. Are you enjoying your stay?"

She snickered.

"I would be enjoying it more if I had someone here in my room to take care of some of my personal needs," she purred.

"Yes, madame, we do offer 24-hour butler service in our royal suites, as you know. Hopefully our butlers can service your every personal need? I'm calling to see if you would like to be the Chef's guest for breakfast this morning here in our private dining room."

"I would love for you to have me for breakfast," said Eva.

"Oui, madame, the pleasure will be mine. Is 7:00 am a good time for you?"

"Perfect," said Eva, smiling, because Charles of course knew she always left the hotel by 8 am.

"Very good, madame. We look forward to seeing you then."

Eva tapped her fingers on the open door of her large closet. She'd have to choose an outfit that could be easily — well, disassembled and reassembled for the corporate law office where she'd be spending the morning after her little breakfast meeting. In the financial fallout of the modern economy, companies rose and fell, and it was her job to deal with multimillion dollar lawsuits between those companies, no matter how exhausting that often was.

Exhausted at work, exhausted at home. Calvin had just come home with his first C, in Biology. She couldn't wait until the day her boys were out of college (*already an optimistic goal*, she thought) and she could get off this hamster wheel, retire, and live on Matthew's Island collecting sea glass and reading whole, actual books like *that* was her career.

But for now, Eva smiled to herself, because at least it looked like it was going to be a panties-in-the-Coach purse kind of morning first.

ZARINA SERVED two mocha lattes to the overwhelmed moms with the unruly looking preschoolers.

She watched as the kids chose from the corner basket containing blocks, puzzles, worn children's board books, and tiny Polly Pocket houses that were once hers. A random My Little Pony or two, some Matchbox cars, and a few Barbie dolls with frazzled hair and frayed princess dresses rounded out the mix of distractions meant to keep kids like these busy so moms could relax and caffeinate.

And for when the moms get desperate? Ring Pops and Fun Dip candies at the counter could keep a kid occupied long enough for his mother to have a gulp or two of some much-needed java. Of course, only the coolest moms let their kids have the sugar. The 'cruncher' moms pulled out a bag of grapes or an organic banana.

Zarina returned to the counter where she was pleased to see one of the moms had placed two Ring Pops, an apologetic look on her face. Zarina smiled at her as Lisa walked in alone.

She looked a little stressed.

"Busy day at the bakery?"

"Yeah, pretty much always," said Lisa, "which I shouldn't complain about."

The shop wasn't busy besides the two moms with their kids, so Zarina asked Lisa if she wanted to sit down and have caramel lattes.

"I'd love that." Lisa looked genuinely happy.

The women had never gotten a chance to sit down and chat, even though the two of them were about as close in age as Lisa was to the other Scarlet Letter Society women.

"So, are you reading *Fear of Flying*?"

"Oh heck yes," said Lisa. "I'm sure I will read all the monthly books, even though we don't really discuss them at our gatherings."

"Can I tell you a little secret?" asked Zarina.

"Sure," said Lisa.

"When I order your books each month, I've been ordering an extra copy for myself and reading along with you."

"That's so funny!" Lisa said, laughing. "Don't worry, I won't tell. So what did you think of the first two books?"

"Well I had read *The Scarlet Letter* in high school, but read it again anyway. And then I really thought *Anna Karenina* was tragic, which is why I thought maybe you guys should skip it."

"I know," said Lisa. "None of these historical books seem to be very understanding towards women who cheat.

I actually think overall that *Anna Karenina* was meant to be a little more on the sympathetic side from Tolstoy's perspective, especially for a man. But there is no doubt it is grim."

"Very true," Zarina said. "I know Maggie read it anyway, but Eva probably won't. You ladies need to find some more uplifting adultery books, that's for sure. Not there are many. *Fear of Flying* should help."

Lisa took out her journal from the nearly-matching preppy Vera Bradley purse and began reading.

"*The zipless fuck is absolutely pure. It is free of ulterior motives. There is no power game. The man is not "taking" and the woman is not "giving." No one is attempting to cuckold a husband or humiliate a wife. No one is trying to prove anything or get anything out of anyone. The zipless fuck is the purest thing there is. And it is rarer than the unicorn. And I have never had one.*"

"Yeah, Erica Jong doesn't really mince words, does she?" Lisa continued, "She goes on to say that the zipless fuck happens because "when you came together, zippers fell away like rose petals, underwear blew off in one breath like dandelion fluff. For the true ultimate zipless A-1 fuck, it was necessary that you never got to know the man very well."

"Do you agree with her?" Zarina asked.

"It's really complex, but truly so simple," said Lisa. "It makes sense that if you had an affair, you would want it to happen in an almost innocent way—not out of spite or anger, but just because two people have come together in a moment in time and had a true connection."

"And they just happened to be married to other people," Zarina said.

Lisa seemed to blush. "Yeah, I mean, that's the catch, right?" said Lisa. "The guilt. If you love your spouse, no matter how imperfect they are, you're still going to feel bad having a relationship with someone else, whether it is a one night stand or a deeper friendship that just morphs into an affair."

Zarina didn't want to pry. Lisa really seemed like she was puzzling this out. It seemed she gave a lot more thought to this stuff than Maggie or Eva, which was probably one reason she didn't open up more around them.

"So have you ever," Zarina asked her, "had a zipless fuck?"

"I guess Jong says they're rarer than a unicorn for a reason," said Lisa, "but yeah, one time in college—isn't that where most zipless fucks happen, right?—I had sex on a boat with a guy whose name I couldn't even tell you today."

Zarina laughed.

"Are you serious? A boat, huh?"

"Yep. I went to culinary school outside DC, but one time we went to a conference in Annapolis," said Lisa. "Our hotel was right on the water at the harbor. I ended up meeting this guy at the bar, and his boat was docked right in front. We went for a ride, and then, well, and then we went for a ride! Sex on a boat was amazing. You can feel the whole boat rocking with the motion of your..."

She couldn't even finish the sentence. She looked up like a kid caught red-handed in a candy store.

Zarina smiled at her. "It's totally cool," Zarina said, pulling her long black hair into a ponytail. Whew! Who knew how hot this coffee chat would be? "I mean, it sounds fantastic."

"It was before I was married," said Lisa.

"And did you end up marrying a guy with a boat?" Zarina asked her jokingly.

Lisa's face relaxed. "Nope. But that probably would have been a really brilliant idea! So what about you, young lady? You're probably too young to ask about such escapades."

"Oh come on, I'm officially old enough to drink legally," Zarina responded. "And I'm certainly not going to be a blushing bride, if I'm ever a bride! Heck yes, I had my college cliché zipless fuck. It was with a girl, and we both had boyfriends at the time. Though it wasn't Stanley. But I think that's what made it zipless—we were both girls, so we didn't have the same guilt as you would if you cheated on your man with another guy."

Zarina had somehow felt necessary to explain to Lisa that she hadn't cheated on Stanley, though it seemed kind of ridiculous under the circumstances of her existing club membership.

"It all goes back to the shame, I think," said Lisa. "Can you live with yourself the next day if you hurt the person you love by being with someone else?"

"I'll leave that question for you, the other members of The Scarlet Letter Society, and Erica Jong to ponder," Zarina said, clearing their cups.

G-Chat With Ron Jacobs
embradley@smithcohenbradley.com
July 5 to Eva

5:02 PM **Ron***: hey*
Eva*: hey!*
Ron*: so have you ever been to a sex club?*
Eva*: um. no*
5:03 PM **Ron***: we should totally go – there is one in Baltimore*
Eva*: have you been there?!*
5:04 PM **Ron***: yeah with Nicole.*
5:05 PM **Eva***: what is it like? And what do u need me to go there for if u have your hot 20something girlfriend already going there with u?*
5:06 PM **Ron***: It's not as freaky as you might think. There are different rooms and you can watch or not watch or go in rooms or not, there's a BYOB bar – it's pretty laid back.*
5:07 PM **Eva***: yeah someone's getting laid there for sure.*
Ron*: truuuuue. haha*

5:08 PM **Eva**: *and you didn't answer...you want me to go to a sex club with you becaussse?*

Ron: *I think u would have fun! Maybe you and Joe could go with me and Nicole.*

5:10 PM **Eva**: *You have obviously lost your mind. Joe and I do not need to be in a sex club to reminded that we don't have sex anymore.. Let me guess — this has something to do with your threesome fantasy, doesn't it...*

Ron: *what! No. Why do u say that!?*

5:11 PM **Eva**: *If you think my forty-one-year-old ass and saggy boobs are EVER going to be naked in front of your perfect little size-zero girlfriend you can dream on, young intern.*

5:12 PM **Ron**: *you wouldn't have to. At a sex club, anything goes.*

Eva: *ew. The concept of the germs alone completely freaks me out.*

5:13 PM **Ron**: *there are pros there to make sure everything is completely sanitized.*

Eva: *ew. They need staff to clean up all the — ew. Just EW.*

5:14 PM **Ron**: *you should just come with me and we can give it a try to see what you think. You might like the "torture chamber" room.*

5:15 PM **Eva**: *Torture chamber sounds fun, I must admit. But not one that someone else was in five* *minutes ago.*

5:17 PM **Ron***: It puts the lotion on its skin or else
it gets the hose again. muahaha*

5:18 PM **Eva***: You are too young for that reference.*

5:19 PM **Ron***: ha ha I think it came out when I was
like in first grade, but I've seen it on AMC.*

Eva*: This conversation is just making me feel old.*

5:20 PM **Ron***: You're not old. You're hot.*

Eva*: So are you, my young staffer. So are you.*

5:21 PM **Ron***: What? Stiffer? Lol Well I surely
look forward to seeing you in the morning.*

Eva*: Yes, see you then. And don't call me Shirley.*

Ron*: Huh?*

Eva*: Nevermind.*

Eva sat back at her kitchen desk area chair, took off her
reading glasses, closed her laptop and wiped her eyes with
her hands, shaking her head. *Yeah, he can maybe get a 90s
Silence of the Lambs reference, but definitely not a 1980 Airplane
reference from four years before he was born!* Having an affair
with someone literally from another decade was interesting,
that was for sure. No Pandora Internet radio station covered
this generation gap.

Although she appreciated Ron's young body, she
constantly felt old and fat and wrinkled around him.
Technically, especially for her age, she wasn't any of those
things—working out paid off, but whenever they were

together, which was rarely in public anyway, she always felt like people (the waiter, the store clerk) looked back and forth quickly between her and Ron in a questioning way. *What is the relationship between these two people?* And it was a fair question.

She sighed. Having had affairs before, she knew the key was to keep the emotion out of them. No "I love you." Saying that or not saying it always seemed to fuck everything up. No promises for the future. *Just enjoy the time you have, don't waste energy being guilty, and don't think too much about the whole thing.* With Charles, she felt more secure because he was older. She wasn't so physically insecure around him. His wife had died of breast cancer, and he was lonely. She filled that physical need for him, and he didn't ask her for more. Their relationship was based on affection, companionship, and fun; the fun for her being the most treasured.

She could hear her teenage sons in the family room playing Call of Duty or Halo or whatever those godforsaken violent video games were that you told yourself as a parent you'd never, ever let your kids play. She remembered not wanting them to play with guns when they were little and wondered where parenting all went to hell. Middle school, she nodded to herself. *Definitely the hormone hell of middle school.*

Joe was in his office in the next room. It was a rare evening when the four of them were home together. Usually, the boys had sports practice or were out with friends, Joe was at the hospital, or she was at the office. The four of them operated pretty independently of one another, but it was dinnertime, so she walked into Joe's office to ask if she should order some Chinese food for delivery. She hated cooking.

She walked in and Joe had stepped out of the room. His laptop was open and she saw the familiar g-chat screen. She wouldn't have noticed it at all, except there was motion on the screen, accompanied by the faint bell sound that indicated a new message.

She didn't mean to snoop; she had just been in the right place at the right time. She saw only a few lines:

> *5:21 PM* **Joe***: Your pussy was so wet this morning.*
> **Kayla***: My body is always ready when I see you. ;)*
> *You were ready too.*
> *5:22 PM* **Joe***: My cock is definitely standing at attention when you enter a room.*
> **Kayla***: Well I can't wait until it enters my room again soon, doctor.*

Then, hearing Joe come back down the hall from the bathroom, she quickly left the room, returning to the kitchen. She felt sick. Forget Chinese food. She told the boys to heat up a frozen pizza and went upstairs to her room, flopping herself on the bed with tears in her eyes. Glancing at her Kindle, she knew losing herself in a few chapters of *Fear of Flying* tonight would help her avoid conversation with Joe. *I am a huge hypocrite to be upset*, she thought. *I was just chatting with my boyfriend moments before.* But something about seeing the sexual chat between her husband and another woman felt like a punch in the stomach.

Why wouldn't he have a girlfriend, she reasoned with herself—a brilliant, handsome doctor in great shape? And God knew he wasn't getting laid at home. She couldn't remember the last time they'd had sex. She couldn't remember the last time they had said "I love you" to one another. Months spilled into years in an unhappy marriage, and there was certainly no point in keeping track.

It was a marriage of convenience, had been from the start, since it took place right after she'd found out she was pregnant with the boys. They'd been dating and were getting along fine. When her diaphragm had failed, and she'd been knocked up, they had made the decision to marry. And now it was all coming back to haunt her.

She looked at Joe's neat side of the nightstand: everything in its place on the dusted table, and her own bedside table, covered in paperwork and moisturizers, charging cords and books. The differences here were the differences between them. He liked things neat, she preferred messy.

She had never felt fulfilled in the marriage--she was starved for love, affection and attention, and the only thing Joe seemed to give attention to was his medical practice. She looked over at the picture on the dresser of her boys on the lacrosse field together. Love and romance had taken a backseat, except where she could find them in an ancillary way around her workplaces.

As a workaholic, it always made sense to Eva that her affairs that revolved somehow around her career. She let her mind wander back to a memory: she'd once fucked a judge in his own chambers after a trial; he was still wearing his robe! She compartmentalized Ron at her office in DC, Charles at her office in New York. Why wouldn't Joe be compartmentalizing someone in Baltimore?

But that doesn't make it hurt any less.

MAGGIE AND Dave finished lunch and the discussion of their daughter's upcoming celebration. She had asked to meet with him, even though a phone call could easily have accomplished the interaction.

Why does it always come back to him? thought Maggie. Entire relationships, marriages, a whole decade between them now, and she never seemed to be able to cut whatever invisible cord kept them coming back together. Then again, he never seemed able to cut that rope, either.

"You have absolutely got to see this fantastic Art Deco building," said Dave. "It's just a few blocks over. Do you have time?"

She did. No one was running a clock on her "Back in an hour" sign at the shop.

Smiling at his child-like excitement over simple old

bricks and mortar, she asked, "So what's the story of this poor unfortunate orphan building?"

"They were going to tear this beauty down," said Dave as they rounded the corner toward the building. He suddenly stopped, pointing. "Just look at her! Original copper and black marble tile façade, even the original Deco lettering."

"They just don't build them like this anymore?" asked Maggie, figuring Dave's signature comment was on its way.

"No one could afford to build a structure like this today," said Dave. He smiled, producing a single key. "Wanna take a look?"

Maggie wasn't as thrilled at the idea of dirty, abandoned buildings as Dave was, but she couldn't resist his enthusiasm. She never could. "Sure," she said, glad she wore vintage jeans for a living and not some Eva-style black skirt get-up.

"It was an old hotel," said Dave as they walked inside. It was dark, musty and dusty like the rest of them, thought Maggie, though she was impressed by the beautiful architecture. The lobby's red, white and black color scheme were all visible again, since the drop ceilings and newer flooring had been removed. Gilded cherubic faces seemed to gleam at her from every corner.

"I love that you do this," said Maggie. "This probably would've ended up some new office building with cubicles and acoustic tile ceilings and blue conference rooms."

"I'm glad it's going to be a hotel again," said Dave. He absentmindedly started rubbing Maggie's shoulders. This turned her to putty and he knew it. She relaxed against his hands, taking in the view of the work in progress around her.

"These old places sure had a lot of charm and romance," said Maggie.

"They still do," said Dave. He turned her toward him, lifted her chin, and kissed her. His beard was rough, but Maggie had grown to like that many years before. She reached up and put her arms around him, savoring the soft familiarity of his flannel shirt. Their kiss grew in intensity and she felt him harden through his jeans. She grabbed his belt and pulled him closer to her.

"You've got to see this elevator," said Dave, pulling Maggie across the lobby by the hand.

They stepped inside the freshly restored 1920s elevator. Maggie noted the deep sound of the "ding" as Dave pushed the number 13.

"It's unusual for a building to have a 13th floor, but the top floor on this one is 13," he said. As the floors rose, he passionately pinned her against the gold corner rail of the elevator. She grabbed his ass, spinning him around and throwing a Converse hi-topped foot on top of the rail, pressing her waist against his jeans to meet his excitement.

Ding.

The doors opened to reveal a giant ballroom spanning the entire thirteenth floor. Huge black marble columns were the only things spanning the expanse. Gilded floor- to-ceiling mirrors covered the walls, except for one entire wall of windows that looked out over the city. Since it was one of the tallest buildings, the view was magnificent. Elegant built-in seats were spaced across the width of the exterior windows.

He scooped Maggie off her feet, twirled her around the dance floor while she laughed, and gently placed her down on one of the window seats. She reached up, undid his belt buckle, and in seconds, they were naked. Their bodies so familiar with one another, yet each completely excited in this new, yet old public space. The possibility of workers appearing to paint or do plumbing was in the back of Maggie's mind, but it didn't stop her.

They made love with Dave kneeling on the window seat and Maggie's ass pressed up against the window. She imagined which other buildings might be "enjoying" this view. After the delicious, frenzied moments of shared passion, she plopped herself down on the window seat and pressed her feet up on the window.

At that exact moment, her phone rang in her pocket. She smiled at Dave, rolling her eyes at the interruption. As she took the phone out of her jeans, which were dusty on the floor, and reached down to turn off the ringer, she heard a voice on the other end and realized she'd accidentally answered it.

"Hello?" asked the phone, with a soft laugh.

"Oh, hey Ted," said Maggie. "I'm just in the middle of something. Let me give you a call back."

She hung up, but when she turned back to Dave she saw the look of hurt in his eyes, regardless of how hard he'd tried to hide it. He dressed quickly.

"No, you go ahead and take your call, Maggie," said Dave. "I really need to get back to the office."

Maggie looked at him. "I didn't mean to answer the damn thing," she said. "I'm sorry. Can't we just pick up where we left off?"

"I don't know, Maggie," said Dave. "Can we? Because your life seems to be pretty full already."

"Aw, Dave, come on, we've never let other people come between us," said Maggie as she dressed; the wide-open nature of the floor plan and lack of heating made the building very chilly.

He didn't speak again, and she could sense he had shut down. He pressed the elevator button, and now the "Ding" of the bell sounded like an accusation to her.

He frowned slightly at her as he turned to leave the building, taking out the key to lock the door behind them.

ZARINA COULDN'T wait to see how this one was going to go. She turned on lights and coffeemakers at Zoomdweebies. She was hoping someone, *anyone* would actually discuss *Fear of Flying* and not blow it off like they did with every other book. *It's completely understandable,* she reasoned, *to get bored by Hawthorne or Tolstoy, with their old-fashioned language,*

but Erica Jong drops f-bombs, masturbation stories and lesbian
fantasies like they're hot. There is just no way in hell those ladies
could pick up those books and put them down again unfinished.
The damn book is even short!

She warmed up the freshly-made blueberry banana
bread as the Scarlet Letter Society women entered and sat at
their usual table.

"He's cheating on me," said Eva, defeated.

Maggie laughed. Eva glared at her. Lisa lowered her eyes.

"Who? *Joe?* So what do you care?" asked Maggie. "You
haven't been in love with your husband in a million years.
Did you think he'd taken a vow of celibacy since the last time
you fucked him, what, two years ago?"

"I still think that would really hurt," said Lisa quietly.

"Well it does, and thank you for understanding, *Lisa*,"
said Eva, narrowing her eyes at Maggie, who rolled hers.
"It sucks. Of course I can't think of a single reason why he
wouldn't be fucking someone else. But when you find it on a
computer screen, it's so raw and sexual and powerful, it just
feels like all the wind's been knocked out of you."

"Aw, I'm sorry, girl, I didn't mean to be insensitive," said
Maggie. "Remember, the whole reason I'm in the middle of
a divorce is because of cheating. And not just my cheating,
but his. Matt wasn't a bad guy, but he couldn't keep it in his
pants. The only one I ever cheated on him with was Dave,
and that doesn't count."

"Wait. WHAT?" said Eva. "You cheated on your second

husband with your first husband?"

"I don't think it counts if you're cheating with your first husband," said Maggie. "It's not like it was a new guy. I didn't start seeing Ted until after Matt and I were separated."

"How long were you sleeping with your ex?" Lisa dared ask.

"Oh, I never stopped fucking Dave," said Maggie. "To this day."

"Holy Mary, Mother of God, Margaret," said Eva. "*Are you completely kidding me?* I can't even understand who you're cheating on *with whom* around here. Didn't you cheat on Dave in the first place during your first marriage, *which you then ended with divorce?* I am so glad Facebook has an "It's Complicated" relationship status for people like you."

"'The bonds of wedlock are so heavy that it takes two to carry them—sometimes three,'" read Lisa from the notes in her worn journal. "It's from *Fear of Flying*. Well, technically it's an Alexandre Dumas quote, but Jong uses it at the beginning of Chapter 8 in *Fear of Flying*."

"Well ain't that the truth," said Maggie. "Dave and I divorced because at the time our marriage couldn't handle the loss of our child. When Brandon died, and we had been through the eighteen months of leukemia treatments, we just had been in mourning too hard and too long for the marriage to handle and we drifted apart. But we never stopped loving each other."

"It does make sense, Maggie. It's not the traditional path,

but it's your path, and it's nothing to be ashamed of. I think it's sweet that you and Dave still connect that way. And guess what? I read the book," said Eva.

"*You read the book?*" asked Lisa and Maggie at the same time.

"Well don't seem so surprised about it," said Eva, smiling. "Although I guess it is technically my first one. Yeah, after I found out Joe was cheating, I just stayed up 'til 3 am reading it."

Zarina set down the plate of warm bread and smiled at Eva.

"I don't mean to eavesdrop, but did I overhear you just say you read the book?"

"She read the book!" said Maggie. "It's a miracle! And we know Lisa read the book, because she took some motherfucking notes in her little notebook here, for cryin' out loud. This will be the actual first book discussion of the Scarlet Letter Society! Hooray for us!"

Zarina looked around at the three women. "I'm glad those book orders are coming in handy. Enjoy your meeting."

Maggie looked at Zarina. "You haven't read *Fear of Flying,* have you, Z?"

"I actually have," said Zarina, adding a small white lie. "For a college women's literature class."

"You should sit down and join us," said Lisa.

"You don't seem like much of a potential club member, but if you'd like to sit in and hang out with us old hags," said

Maggie, "we'd love to have a young hipster like yourself for the first time."

Zarina sat down, excited to join the ladies. "I cheated on my college boyfriend with a girl one time," she said. "I mean, if that is good enough for a one-time guest pass into SLS."

"Is it even cheating if it's with a girl?" said Eva, laughing.

"It's close enough," said Maggie, smiling. "It barely passes as cheating because when the guy finds out, he usually just thinks it's hot and wants to watch, that's all."

The women laughed.

"So, who wants to talk about the zipless fuck first?" said Maggie.

"I think it's a conundrum, almost an oxymoron," started Lisa. "Jong defines the zipless fuck as sex with no consequences, but in order to have sex in the first place, zippers are coming down."

"I just love Isadora Wing so much," said Eva. "She's the best feminine literary character I've ever encountered."

"That is possibly because she's the first literary character you've ever encountered," joked Maggie. "Just kidding. Well obviously she's my favorite, since I named children and businesses after her. I love her strength. And her admission of weakness. I love her humanity."

Lisa read from her journal.

"'We drove to the hotel and said goodbye. How hypocritical to go upstairs with a man you don't want to fuck, leave the one you do sitting there alone, and then, in a state of great excitement, fuck the one you don't want to fuck while pretending he's the one you do. That's called fidelity. That's called monogamy. That's called civilization and its discontents.'"

"That is some complicated shit," said Zarina. "I love Jong's honesty. She's a pioneer. For 1973, this book is a groundbreaker. Any bullshit literary criticism it received came from the male-dominated mindset held even by some overly old-fashioned women who obviously weren't getting laid."

"She definitely wasn't afraid to say what women were thinking in the 70s," said Eva. "And she said it with great style."

"I like the tug-of-war Isadora has within herself," Lisa said. "It's so raw and genuine. Her perspective is so unique and interesting to experience. You genuinely care about what happens to her, even though she's a fictional character. I felt like she was real."

"Well there has always been a lot of discussion about how much Erica Jong there is in Isadora Wing," said Maggie. "That may be why the character is so real—because in some ways, she is real. You know, the whole 'all fiction is nonfiction' thing."

"What did you think about the ending?" asked Eva. "I felt like I wanted it to be more Hollywood—the big embrace."

"But we know that in the end, even in the end of a book that is all about sex, in the end she chooses love," said Lisa.

"Ok, one more quote, and then I promise I'll stop: 'Do you want me to tell you something really subversive? Love is everything it's cracked up to be. That's why people are so cynical about it. It really is worth fighting for, being brave for, risking everything for. And the trouble is, if you don't risk anything, you risk even more.' "

"We all cheat for a reason," said Maggie. "And it's usually because we feel like we're missing love. Jong lays that out. Call us a whore or a slut or sew a goddamn scarlet letter on our damn t-shirt if you want, but at the end of the day, we all just want to go to bed with someone who makes us feel loved, and wake up next to that same person the next morning."

"Yeah," said Eva. "It just sucks that love is a complete pain in the ass sometimes."

The women laughed softly, and knowingly.

August 2012

"There's just this empty place inside of me that only he can fill."
-"Torn Between Two Lovers," Mary MacGregor

Monthly meeting of the Scarlet Letter Society.
Zoomdweebies Café
Friday, August 3, 2012
5:30 a.m.

You're off the hook. Everyone traveling and whatnot, so this month we will take a "book club" summer vacation. Too hard to follow Erica Jong anyway.

"The scarlet letter was her passport into regions where other women dared not tread."--*The Scarlet Letter*, Nathaniel Hawthorne

"*S*o how'd your Ho-prah book club meeting go?" asked Wes as he sifted through the rack of vintage 1960s men's t-shirts at Maggie's shop.

Maggie stood at the counter, pricing a box of women's shoes from the 1940s. She smiled.

"It was quite intellectual, asshole," she said. "We actually talked about a book."

"Oh, I thought the whole "book club" thing was just to make you all feel like you were actually doing something productive, but that you never actually read any of the books," Wes said.

"To be honest, that's what usually happens. But I think we needed to get away from the historical shit. While it is beautifully written, it was just too long-winded for the likes of us, possibly with the exception of Lisa, who I think was probably the only one who read it."

"The cute piemaker! I'm so proud of her," said Wes. "I'm going to go over there and buy a blackberry pie from her, and then give it to my mother because it's too fattening."

"Yeah, God forbid you eat too many carbs, even when there's fruit involved," said Maggie.

"What did you just call me?" Wes huffed in mock disgust.

"I need advice," said Maggie.

"Oh, God. Well let me guess," said Wes. "Even though I'm your gay best friend, you are once again going to seek my Yoda-like Jedi wisdom on straight men and sex and dating."

"Pretty much," said Maggie. "I think it was re-reading

Fear of Flying again that got me into this 'thinking about my love life' mode, and now I'm just kind of a mess."

"Oh, God, you read *Fear of Flying* again. Ok, Isadora, well, what the hell exactly is your problem?"

"I don't know. I just feel like such a relationship failure. I fucked up my first marriage, then I fucked up my second marriage. Now I have a boyfriend and a girlfriend...and Dave and I just fucked."

"I'm sorry. I clearly did not hear you. *Whaaat* did you just say?" asked Wes, surprised.

"We had lunch plans to talk about Lilith's graduation party," said Maggie. "I don't even know how it ended up happening. He wanted to show me this historic building in town that he'd just saved from the wrecking ball and listed on the National Register of Historic Places. So we walked the few blocks over there after lunch. I said I'd love to see the inside, and he of course knew which door to go in, and we ended up fucking on this huge windowsill on the 13th floor. Half the town could probably see us."

"You. Have. Got. To. Be. Fucking. Kidding. Me," said Wes. "Exhibitionism is a new one for you. And who fucks on the 13th floor? Have you and Dave ever hooked up since your divorce? I *know* you would've told me."

"Oh, hell yeah," said Maggie. "I didn't tell anyone, I was so embarrassed! Just told the girls at A-club group therapy. I totally cheated on my second husband with Dave, who was cheating on his second wife with me before they divorced.

We've gotten together on and off over the years since our divorce."

"Well I do declare, Margaret," said Wes, "this is an entirely different shade of scarlet!"

"I know," said Maggie. "I guess I never felt like it was cheating if it was Dave. We have kids together. We have history. Our marriage fell apart because we lost our son, and we just didn't know how to console each other or even ourselves. But I never stopped loving him."

"Oh my Holy God," said Wes. He put two bowling shirts on the counter and took out his wallet. "Alfred and I will look fab in these at 50s night at the theatre. Girl, you're a hot mess as usual. I'm not even sure what advice to give you, and you know I'm never speechless. I guess to me it sounds like eventually you and Dave are going to have to sit down, in a chair, not on each other's faces, and talk about what the hell is going on."

"You're right," said Maggie. "At some point I'm going to have to learn to stop putting band aids on the gaping wound from my first marriage ending. It's not fair to the band aid people. But I don't know how Dave feels. I always figured maybe it's just a sex thing for him—he's a guy!"

"Well, I'm a guy, and I'm as much of a fan of random sex as the next guy, but I don't think that is what is going here," said Wes. "Remember what you said before about having these other people be "fillers" and now you're calling them "band aids" or whatever. I know that feeling from my past relationships, and it's what's different about the one I'm in now. Maybe the only thing that can heal that wound is going to come right from the source of it."

"I don't know," said Maggie. "I guess time will tell."

"It always does, honey," said Wes, giving Maggie a big hug.

LISA NERVOUSLY sprayed glass cleaner on the front window of the bakery. The tiny café set in the shop's bay window was a perfect place for a mom to sit with her three-year-old and a scone, but while she texted on her phone, the three-year-old had pawed the front windows with chocolate milk fingers, watching the cars and people go by.

Ben would be there shortly. She had offered to make lunch, but he had insisted on bringing it, noting that she cooked for people all day and deserved the break. He was picking up food from the great Thai restaurant up the road.

The bakery was open, so she wasn't nervous about getting into an awkwardly sexual interaction that she confusingly both wanted and didn't want to happen. She slumped into the café chair. *What exactly is it that you do want, Lisa? The* voice in her head asked her. *Do you want him to take you in the back and throw you over the sofa, like you told the Scarlet Letter Society he already has? Or do you just want friendly conversation and flirtation and another round with your vibrator later on, thinking of him while Jim is at work?*

She'd written one thought in her journal that morning that seemed to be one of the only truths she knew at this point: "*He takes away the loneliness.*" It was a powerful thing. Even in a marriage, it was shocking how lonely you could actually feel sometimes.

She finished cleaning the fingerprints on the window. She had felt sorry for the little girl whose mother had been so distracted by her iPhone. Was texting or checking your email really more important that the adorable, curly-headed little blonde girl sitting across from you? Lisa knew she wasn't someone who should judge a mother, not being one herself, but the jealousy over wanting to be a mother sometimes made her critical of women who seemed to take for granted the gift of a beautiful child.

And then she saw Ben walking up the street. He hadn't seen her yet. He wore faded jeans, worn loafers, and a slightly wrinkled dark green polo shirt, the neck of a white t-shirt showing beneath it. His brown crew cut hair was neat as always. In addition to a large brown paper bag containing their lunch, he carried a folder of logo illustrations.

She scurried back behind the counter and busily put freshly baked muffins into the shop's front case. The bell above the Victorian building's old original double front doors jingled as he entered, smiling at her. She returned the smile, feeling color rise to her cheeks and willing it to fade back down.

"Good afternoon, Ms. Swain," said Ben.

"Well good afternoon, Mr. Nidale," said Lisa, trying not to grin like a middle school girl with a crush on the boy in her algebra class.

Lisa realized that since most of their communications had taken place on electronic devices (in addition to the fantasy sequences scrawled in her journal) this was one of the few times they'd actually met in person, and she was nervous. She knew more about him from stalking him on Facebook (status says single, photos with girl say "maybe girlfriend?") than she did about actually sitting across from him at a table and having a conversation. And as he placed the lunch bag on the table, she realized how small it was. The tiny round iron table had been picked because it fit in the small window space with two matching chairs; an adorable vintage set from one of many nearby antique shops. Now they'd be eating messy food with chopsticks practically on top of each other

These thoughts didn't help with her nervousness, so she set about preparing for their meal. She asked Ben if iced tea was okay (sweet, of course, since they were below the Mason Dixon line, if only barely). He indicated that it was and she poured their drinks.

Ben started pulling things out of the bag and held up the file folder.

"I don't think we can manage to eat all this food and have this meeting at the same time. I propose lunch first, then meeting," said Ben.

"Agreed," said Lisa, trying to control her grin.

They sat down to eat, Lisa finding herself with the rare hope that customers would magically manage to stay away for just a little while.

"Thank you so much for bringing lunch by," said Lisa, trying to break the awkward silence as the pair sort of gazed at each other. "This is definitely a treat. I usually eat a day-old scone for lunch."

"The loveliest baker in town should not have to eat day-old bread," said Ben, his smile revealing a dimple on one cheek that for some reason seemed directly connected to a nerve inside her nipples.

She blushed again and looked down at her shrimp Pad Thai. She'd been too embarrassed to admit to Ben that she hated spicy food—she had learned over time that when stuck in a Thai restaurant with friends that this was the safe, non-spicy dish.

"It's delicious," said Lisa.

"It's my son's favorite," said Ben. "He won't eat the spicy stuff."

Lisa looked up from her plate and was unable to mask the complete surprise from her face.

Ben laughed. "I didn't think I'd had a chance to mention him. Max is four. He is from a previous relationship; we never married. I get to spend time with him a few times a month. He's fantastic."

"Oh! I bet he's great," said Lisa, mentally going through Facebook pictures and not remembering seeing a child. "To be really honest, I'm jealous. I've been trying for a few years to get pregnant, but with no luck."

"Sounds like you and your husband really want a child?" said Ben.

"I've always wanted to be a mother," said Lisa. "I think Jim wants a baby, too, but he definitely isn't as enthusiastic as I guess I am, especially the more time that goes by."

"Well, you're still really young," said Ben. "I'm sure it will work out."

And he smiled at her with his brown-green-*what-the-hell-color-is-that* eyes, and she felt guilty for feeling that smile all the way in the middle of her. Part of her, probably an unknowing biological, basic animal instinct part, wanted nothing more than fertile sperm so she could have the baby she wanted. She imagined hurling all the food across the shop and jumping on the iron table, yanking him to a standing position and wrapping her legs around him so she could feel his desire as she licked his neck and breathed in the smell of whatever that goddamn amazing man-perfume smell was.

She swallowed hard, and took a drink of tea.

"Are you okay?" asked Ben.

"Yes, sorry, just daydreaming," she said. "And is it hot in here?"

"It's just you," said Ben, smiling. "Penny for your thoughts." He reached into a pocket and somehow produced an actual penny, which he placed on the table.

Lisa didn't know what to say. *Well, my thoughts are that*

I wish you would completely ravage me right now in my shop window? Somehow that seemed inappropriate. But only because it would be a complete disaster if a customer walked in. The back room couch? Totally doable.

She sighed.

"Honestly, I'm not sure my thoughts are appropriate in a place of business during a business meeting," said Lisa in a mock-serious tone of voice.

Ben laughed. "Inappropriate thoughts can be the most fun kind," he said. "But I absolutely do not want you to be concerned about the professionalism of this meeting. So should we get started?"

He picked up the file folder from the windowsill.

Lisa smiled. "Yes, of course we should, graphic design consultant. Let's get right down to business."

Eva unlocked the door of her hotel room, putting down her purse and suitcase and flopping onto the soft living room sofa. As unpleasant as her firm's pending court case was going to be, she was glad she had to travel to New York this week. As was often the case lately, work was going to be a great escape from her personal life. She couldn't wait to get on the DC train and away from Joe. She'd completed reviewing the case during the Acela train ride so she could relax for a few hours when she arrived in the city.

She'd managed to collect herself on that night enough

not to discuss her discovery with her husband, but she'd thought of little else for the past few days. Somehow, she knew it was a game changer. The boys were in high school now, and even as immaturely as they sometimes acted, she knew they didn't need her in the same way as the days when she was packing peanut butter and jelly and Capri Suns in lunchboxes (or the au pair was). So why was she staying in a dead marriage? What were they waiting for to separate? The boys to leave for college?

She wanted a drink. The bar was of course already stocked with her favorite wines, and she selected a bottle of strawberry wine from the Maryland vineyard Linganore Wine Cellars, marveling at how much attention the hotel paid to detail.

Eva's love life was a mystery to her. *Why do I need two men to make me feel fulfilled? One in each city? Really? Gah. It's not really fair to either of them.* She knew she wasn't really committed, especially to Ron. The poor kid was born in the 80s, and the entire relationship was basically nothing more than a hot-for-teacher crush. The sex was great, there was no doubt about that. She definitely understood the cougar relationship appeal now, but she still felt empty emotionally. It wasn't like Ron was ever going to look her in the eyes and tell her that he was madly in love with her.

And that seemed to be what she wanted from someone. Or was it?

I hate the idea of depending on a man for happiness, she

thought, opening the wine.

So what about Charles? They'd been seeing each other for seven months, a natural enough timeframe for two people in a relationship to start asking what the hell was happening, right? Charles had been the proverbial tough nut to crack, though. His wife's death was still recent enough that Eva knew he didn't seem ready to enter any type of serious relationship, which was perfect, since neither did she. But the more time that went by, the more connected she seemed to feel to him. It was almost like she was using Ron as insurance against falling in love with Charles and getting hurt. *What a complete mess,* she thought. But she decided she wasn't going to let it get to her.

She picked up her wine glass and walked out onto the terrace of her suite, to take in the summer view of Central Park. It was sticky, humid August hot like only New York City could be, but there was a slight breeze, and the cool air sucked out of the suite and refreshed her. She watched the couples ride the horse drawn carriages. *Clippity-clop, clippity-clop.* The horses' hooves clopped on and on, day after day in Central Park. She watched a couple snuggle as the weary horse carried them past benches where homeless people slept at night. *Living the dream,* she thought sardonically.

She felt her phone vibrate in the pocket of her jeans.

"New message from Charles" lit up as she looked at the screen.

Charles: *Join me in the Palm Court dining room*
for dinner at 7, madame?
Eva: *Bien sur, monsieur.*
Charles: *Parfait. Comme nous.*
Eva: *Merci!*

She smiled. She certainly didn't think she was perfect, but the dinner plans sounded perfectly like what she needed. She walked back inside, pouring another glass of wine. *I deserve it*, she thought. *I'm just going to have one more glass, to relax.* She used to have carefully set up rules about not drinking when she was alone (*I will not end up an alcoholic like my father*), but those had been rationalized away over recent years.

I need to sink myself into a hot bath. Even though it was hot outside, she needed heat for her aching muscles. Her trips to the gym were more frequent lately as she found things to fill empty moments. In the bathroom, an enormous, elegant basket filled with scented bath salts and aromatherapy oils awaited her. She lit two lavender eucalyptus candles and chose tangerine ginger Dead Sea bath salts to toss into the steaming water as it rose. She added a few drops of eucalyptus oil to the water; the oil reversed the drying effect a bath could have on her skin. There were no windows in the master suite's bathroom, so when she closed the door and turned the lights off, the room was dark. She breathed in the glorious smell from the eucalyptus oil and felt her shoulders relax.

Eva ran her hand across the soft Plaza robe hanging on the beautiful antique hook, setting the matching slippers on the plush area rug beside the tub.

She tested the water with her toe. It was the perfect bath temperature—hot enough that you'd have to get in slowly; not too cool to lose its heat while you soaked. The scents of the herbs and fruits from her candles and sea salts had blended perfectly. She placed her wine glass beside the tub and slowly sunk into the steaming, therapeutic waters that awaited her.

As she floated there, Eva's thoughts continued to plague her. As much as she would love to push images of her life's unfolding dramas aside and just relax and enjoy the moment, there was nothing like lying in a hot bath to clear your thoughts.

And then Eva started to cry. The darkness, the silence, the intense smells, the heat, the wine, but especially the *aloneness* in light of the discovery of her husband's affair, just all hit her at once. She cried. It was the kind of deep, gasping cry that you couldn't stop if you wanted to. It wracked her small body and she just had to surrender to it. Tears poured from her like the water from the gold faucet; they filled the tub together. She cried for not feeling like a good mother, not being a good wife. She cried from the stress of her job. She cried because her love life was so complicated. And she cried because at the end of the day, she just wanted to be happy.

After an hour of soaking and crying and wine, Eva managed to collect herself, splashed cold water on her face, and started getting ready for her dinner with Charles. She was starving, hadn't eaten all day, and looked forward to whatever culinary treats he had in store for her.

She chose a pale blue short-sleeved Ann Taylor sweater and a vintage rust orange leather miniskirt she'd bought at Maggie's shop. She wore simple square diamond earrings and a plain silver chain with a matching diamond pendant. Her husband may have been bad at many things, but selecting jewelry on holidays and her birthday was not one of them. She sprayed three puffs of Coach Poppy perfume into the air and walked through the small cloud. Her Sephora makeup was expertly applied; she was a fan of the brand and knew which color combinations flattered her hair and eye colors. Dark copper spiked Christian Louboutin heels completed the outfit. With her small stature she was used to wearing very high heels, but that didn't make her any less grateful for elevators and the fact that she'd be dining in the building she was already in.

She exited the luxurious elevator at the main level of the hotel. She raised her head to marvel at the opulence of the architecture. It was no wonder the building had been chosen as a setting by F. Scott Fitzgerald for *The Great Gatsby*.

She stopped in front of the Palm Court dining room, because a "Closed for Private Event" sign greeted her. She tried the door. It was locked. A waiter instantly appeared beside her.

"Follow me, madame," he said.

She did.

Taking her around to another, non-public entrance, he held the door open for her and she entered the opulent room. The waiter left and she walked further into it. Large opaque white silk screens had been placed in front of the room's huge arched windows, creating a completely private space. In addition to the giant palm trees that were the room's moniker, there was only a single table for two set in the middle of the room under the magnificent arched stained glass ceiling. At least a hundred peach-colored candles in every height, shape and size illuminated the room. The electric lights had been turned down to accent the candles' glow. The table was stunning. In the center was a five-foot high-stemmed vase with a spray of lilies in every color, their smell filling the air.

This is a room where a wedding should be taking place right now, instead of a dinner for two, she thought. She felt completely underdressed in her sweater and skirt.

She gasped as she stood and appreciated the sights within the gorgeous room. She heard a door open and felt Charles walk into the room behind her. She turned and ran into his arms. He chuckled.

"This is the most amazing, beautiful room I've ever seen in my life," she said, and she struggled to fight back tears as she squeezed him in a thankful embrace.

"I was so happy to do it for you, Eva," said Charles. He straightened his arms, held her slight waist, and looked straight into her eyes with his own dark brown ones.

"I have a four-course meal planned for you, madame," he said. "So I hope that you are hungry."

"Absolutely starving, Chef," she said, smiling up at him. Even in her three-inch platform heels, he was a few inches taller. He returned her smile, gesturing towards the elegant dining table.

"Shall we?" he said.

"I believe we absolutely shall," she said.

They sat, and as if on cue, a waiter entered with drinks. Her favorite, champagne with Chambord raspberry liqueur for her, a glass of red something-he-probably-picked-to-go-with-the-meal for him. Jazz music played softly in the background.

"I can't believe you did all this for me," said Eva.

"It was fun," said Charles. "I'm so glad you like it. I hope you enjoy the meal I have prepared for you. I'm trying out some new culinary experiments."

"That sounds exciting," said Eva, sipping from her sweet pink bubbles.

"I think it will be," said Charles, with a lazy smile. He sipped his wine and admired the beautiful woman who sat before him. The door opened again, and another waiter entered with two small plates.

"Amuse-bouche," said the waiter, placing the plates in

front of them. "A gift from the chef."

"This whole evening is a lovely gift from the chef," replied Eva, gazing across the table at her dark-haired lover. She knew, because he was near obsessive compulsive about his selections of food and style of dining, that this entire evening, down to the timed entries of each waiter, had been meticulously planned for days. And she was thankful for it. *What an amazing escape*, she thought.

They ate the duck confit together in silence. He knew duck was one of her favorites. Plates entered and disappeared as if by magic—baked oysters with prosciutto and champagne cream, pan-seared petit filet mignon. It never occurred to Eva whether the foods were in season, and how much trouble Charles had to go through to get some of them. She was stuffed, and delightfully so.

Another glass of Champagne and Chambord arrived without the need for her to request it.

"And now it is almost time for dessert," said Charles, and he stood up.

She smiled and asked, "Are we going somewhere else for dessert?"

"Not far," he replied, taking her hand. She stood.

He led her to another area that had been prepared to appear like a small sitting room. An antique French sofa, coffee table, and two plush chairs were gathered on a beautiful Persian rug. More candles lit the area, and a bowl of roses was centered on the coffee table with a grouping of candles.

"This is beautiful," said Eva.

"As are you," said Charles. He walked over and sat on the sofa. She left her heels on the rug and sunk into the cushions, tucking her feet under her. Another waiter appeared. He brought a covered silver dish, placing it on the table before them, and disappeared as quickly as he had arrived.

"That will be our last interruption for the evening," said Charles. They heard the click of the door when the waiter left.

"Is this some kind of surprise dessert?" said Eva.

"Yes, it is a new recipe I am trying," said Charles. He lifted up the silver platter's cover to reveal a bed of Pop Rocks candy packets in every flavor, with two crystal dishes of sorbet placed amongst them. Eva laughed.

"Pop Rocks?" she said.

"Yes, Pop Rocks," responded Charles. "A few weeks ago I overhead two of the waitresses talking about their favorite candies as children. One of them mentioned these things — Pop Rocks? And I had never heard of them. The other girl told me how delicious they were, and one day she brought in a packet of them. Watermelon. I tried them. And they are delicious."

"We all loved them as kids," said Eva, grinning. "And watermelon has always been my favorite."

"I decided to try to make sorbet with them," said Charles, "because I thought the culinary surprise of the popping combined with the intense flavor would be enjoyable in a frozen form. And so — voila! Watermelon Pop Rocks sorbet."

She picked up her spoon and silver bowl and dug in. As soon as the frozen, carbonated watermelon magic hit her tongue, she giggled like a little girl.

"Oh my God, this is the most delicious thing ever."

"I'm so glad you think so," said Charles. He reached over, picked up a packet of Watermelon Pop Rocks, and sprinkled some on the top of each of their bowls. "The finishing touch."

"Another bizarre thought about the Pop Rocks came into my mind," said Charles. "And I would like to try that as well." Raising a spoonful of the candy from its silver bowl, he took a mouthful of the candy, and leaned over to kiss Eva. She could feel the popping of the candy as soon as his lips touched hers. She instinctively opened her mouth. As their tongues met, the Pop Rocks sizzled and fizzed and popped audibly, and she wondered how she had existed for four decades without Pop Rocks kisses.

She put down her bowl and picked up a spoonful of strawberry Pop Rocks; there was a silver bowl of each flavor. "Have you tried the strawberry?" she asked.

"Yes, and it is also delicious," said Charles. "Which is a word that reminds me of you."

He took Eva in his arms and kissed her passionately, but she pushed him away playfully and filled her mouth with a spoonful of the strawberry Pop Rocks. Then, she kissed him back. She let some of the candy remain on her tongue as she licked his ear. He shuddered at the sound of the candy popping in his ear combined with the sensation of her tongue. He was already hard.

Eva reached down and felt his rising arousal.

"I think you like strawberry, too," she said.

His large, strong hands slid underneath her sweater, running gently up her sides. She sighed. His hands gently caressed the outside of her pale teal silk bra, and her nipples rose to greet his fingers. He unfastened her bra. He lifted her sweater gently over her head. Placing her firmly onto the pillow at the corner of the couch, he caressed her breasts, teasingly moving his hands down her waist to where he knew she wanted them.

Her bra hit the floor as he picked up a spoonful watermelon Pop Rocks and took a mouthful. When his lips took in her breast, she arched her back and let out a tiny squeal. The sensation of the carbonated candy on her nipples was unprecedented. There was a slight grittiness to the texture of the small crystals as his tongue circled her nipples, and the popping from within his mouth felt amazing on her tender flesh.

As he continued to incorporate Eva's breasts into the dessert menu, he reached down between her legs. He was delighted to find that as usual, she wore no panties. When his right hand reached her, she was already wet for him. He hiked up her skirt for better access, teasing her with his agile thumb. She softly moaned, clawing at his shirt. She wanted him naked. She wanted him to fuck her more than she had wanted any other part of this meal.

But he was taking his time. He was the one in charge of this course, and he would design its presentation. He continued sucking at her nipples and letting her feel his desire on the inside of her thigh. She pressed her inner thigh against his stiffness, running her hand on the outside of his pants and making him sigh out loud. He returned her hand to her side firmly. He unzipped her skirt and removed it so that she was fully naked, seemingly unaffected by the fact that she was currently without clothes in one of the busiest restaurants in New York City, where hundreds had dined that day and every day for more than a century.

He grabbed the bowl of Tropical Punch Pop Rocks and looked down at her.

"I'm ready for my dessert now," he said. He slowly poured small spoonfuls of candy onto her belly and inner thighs. While she laughed, lazily circling her own nipple and licking the remaining candy from her sticky fingers, he poured the remainder into his own mouth. And as he lowered his head to lick her with his mouthful of popping candy, her hips rose to meet his fizzing tongue.

She moaned, and was able to utter the words, "I think Tropical Punch is my new favorite flavor."

ZARINA CLAMBERED into the shop early on the first Friday of

the month. She swept up and straightened the place, picking up a few random Legos on the floor from yesterday's kid visitors. She hooked up her iPhone to the speaker set and put the 80s station on Pandora, but not too loud, just so it created a nice background vibe.

As she swept, she thought about how Stanley had been so supportive of her busy life, between the graduate journalism class at the college and running the shop. He'd jokingly said, *"I'm just worried that if you become too educated, you'll reject my alternative lifestyle record shop immaturity."* She laughed and told him being a hipster was not an alternative lifestyle because it was far too underground to be that mainstream.

She finished mixing the muffins and put them in the oven, so it would smell good when the women came in, and thought about how she hated feeling like she depended on a guy for anything. *How do you make it work in relationships*, she wondered, *so that you need the person, and they know you need them so they don't just go take off and hang out with someone else, but they don't think you need them too much so that you're needy?*

Forget saying "I love you." Her generation knew better than that. *Not just because we're too spoiled and lazy to bother falling in love with someone other than ourselves,* Zarina thought. Many of their generation's parents had gotten divorced in dramatic and disastrous ways, and the younger crowd seemed to prefer to avoid marriage to stay away from those situations altogether.

Zarina's parents had just sort of always been happy together, she thought, as she absentmindedly started a second pot of coffee. Not head over heels in love, really openly, but they had a quiet sense of love about them that made their companionship completely natural. That's what Zarina wanted. *Call it love or don't,* thought Zarina. *I just want someone to curl up on the couch and watch a horror movie with, or eat crabby Eggs Benedict and hash browns on a Sunday. Or even just sit next to each other while working on laptops, our legs touching just that little bit, just to say, you know, I'm glad you're here.*

For now, that was Stanley for her. So she felt lucky.

"Good morning, gorgeous!" said Maggie in that boisterous New England accent. She went over and hugged Zarina. "Good to see you. You know what? I'm going to try something new for a change. Give me an iced chai latte, please."

Maggie smiled at Zarina and thought about how she'd just made out with Z's mother, Kate, the day before. She blushed, wondering how those paths were eventually going to cross and what would happen if they did. She didn't want things to be awkward at Zoomdweebies, and she wasn't really sure how things were going to go with Kate. *Ah, the tangled webs.*

"Whoa, there, branching out are we?" Zarina said. "Life's too short not to try a new kind of coffee once in awhile, right?"

"I agree," said Maggie, with an odd half-grin.

"That is absolutely true," said Lisa as she walked in.

"Good morning, Zarina. I'll try an iced chai latte too."

"Well change certainly makes the world go 'round," said Zarina. "I certainly hope you're going to at least try these pineapple coconut muffins I made for you."

"Oh, I bet those are low fat," said Maggie, squinting and scrunching up her face.

"Of course they are," says Zarina. "I mean, pineapples and coconuts are fruits. It's only when you ask for the muffin warmed up with butter melted all over it that it gets a tad more caloric."

"Well, why in the hell else would you eat the damn thing?" said Maggie.

"Those sound amazing," said Lisa. "I think I need to buy a dozen extra of those for my shop today—it will seem like I already made them. I have a ton of pie orders today, so if you don't mind, that would be great. Of course I'll give you credit. We can call them Z muffins."

"Perfect," Zarina said. "Anytime you need some back up baked goods, let me know."

"That's truly an amazing concept," said Lisa. "I'll absolutely take you up on it. So where's Eva today?"

"You won't believe it. She's not coming," said Maggie. "She just texted me late last night. I didn't get the message 'til this morning. She stayed in New York."

"What? Was she supposed to come back last night?" asked Lisa.

"Yeah, she always takes the same train back," said

Maggie. "And she didn't give me any more details. I texted her this morning, but I haven't heard back. It must be a work thing."

"Or a Charles thing," said Lisa.

Maggie's eyes widened. "You think so? I've never known her once to change her plans for a man."

"You never know," said Lisa. "A damn man can make you do things you don't necessarily like to admit you wanted."

"Well isn't that the damn truth?" said Maggie.

Zarina walked over to deliver the warm buttered muffins and iced chai lattes to the brown leather couch area where Maggie and Lisa were hunkered down.

"Mind if I sit for a minute?" she asked.

"Of course," said Maggie.

"You know you don't even need to ask," said Lisa.

Zarina replied, "I know I'm not a member of the society. I always feel like maybe I should run out and cheat on Stan one night so I could feel more like I fit in."

"You know our group name is more for fun," said Maggie. "The very word 'society' is so not us that it's not even funny. It's a lot more casual than that. We only picked the title because Eva and I were joking one day about the 'Red Hat Society' that the older women have and we said 'we should have a red A society.'

"But basically we're just women who get together and talk about shit, and sometimes that shit is about sleeping around, and sometimes it's not. Today, for example. Watch me change the subject so we're not even talking about cheating and men. Today, I would like to talk about what goddamn thundercunts some women can be."

Lisa and Zarina laughed. *"Thundercunts?"* they both said at the same time.

"Ah, yeah, it's one of my old faves," said Maggie. "If I find myself overusing it too much, I'll hit 'Cuntasaurus Rex', which is Eva's fave, though she's never been much of a champion cusser like myself. To me, the old 'thundercunt' is a staple for a woman who has truly earned it."

"I'm always just afraid the c-word is so offensive to women," said Lisa, blushing slightly. "I mean, I'm not a big cusser either."

"Nah, fuck that. Women can call the "c" card with other women when there are simply no other words to use. It's not like I'm goddamn anti-feminist, and it's also not my fault our shitty language doesn't have enough words to cover some of these C-rexes."

"So who pissed you off?" Zarina asked.

"There's this bitch that comes into my shop," said Maggie. "And she does nothing but complain. *'Can you come down on the price of these shoes? Is there a stain on this 1960s skirt, because it should be marked down? Why are you only open 'til 5 on Sundays?'* It's always fucking *something*. Week after week she comes in, always negative. It makes me hate being in retail, which I normally don't mind at all. And does she ever really spend any money? Of course not. She's so rude to me, and miserable. I don't even know why she comes in. She has a scowl on her face from the moment the door opens. And in her stupid blond bob and preppy Lily Pulitzer outfit, she doesn't even wear the kind of clothes I sell! It's like she sucks all the air out of the room. SHE, my friends, is a thundercunt."

"I hear you," said Zarina. "Working in customer service can completely suck. There's a woman whose coffee is never, ever right. She's mean, always in a hurry, and never happy. I would say she would be on my 'Thundercunt of the Month' chalkboard if I had one in the shop, which maybe I should!"

Lisa laughed. "How funny would that be? Like a Wanted poster, with a frowny photograph and name of the "T.C" of the month. I've been really lucky at the bakery. I have people bitch and moan, but no diehard thundercunts so far. But at home? In my subdivision? Oh my God, I think it's the land of Thundercuntopia, and there would be some serious competition for Queen over there. Who has the best landscaping, who has the nicest "builder upgrades," you name it. I actually had my pool membership revoked last summer because I planted tulips around a tree without getting permission from the landscaping committee."

"Yeah, if you're on the landscaping committee of a homeowner's association in a subdivision?" said Maggie. "You're pretty much a guaranteed t-cunt by default. No question."

"And the women are so phony," continued Lisa,

obviously on a roll. "It's like they're judging you every second. The ones who seem nice and then you find out later talk about you behind your back—they're the worst. I know they have some secrets of their own over there, too. But really, you want to say something about me? Say it to my face, you cowardly bitch!"

Zarina laughed. "Lisa, I have to say, I don't think I've ever heard you curse so much!"

Lisa's faced flushed. "I'm sorry," she said. "I just can't stand women who are fake. It's like they pretend to have these perfect lives, and it's all a façade. They're really miserable, so they just make other people miserable, all while hosting the most beautiful party in the neighborhood. All while going to church and then also drinking tons of wine every day, of course."

"You don't need to be sorry," said Maggie. "Subdivision living leaves a lot to be desired, which is why most of us are townies. Sure, there are cliques in town, too, and believe you me, those bitches beat all—you think a homeowner's association is bad, you should see the madness in a historic district commission. But at least in town there's more of a blend of people, so you can avoid the t-cunts as much as possible."

"Well, I guess I don't have to worry about cheating on Stan to have something to talk about at this meeting," said Zarina.

"Nah, sometimes it's nice just to blow off some steam

with some cool girls," said Maggie.

"That," said Lisa, "is absofuckinglutely the truth!"

And the three women laughed, savoring their coffee until it was time to return to the real world outside.

September 2012

"Am I wrong to hunger for the gentleness of your touch? Knowin' you've got someone else at home who needs you just as much? If I can't see you when I want to, I'll see you when I can."
-"If Loving You is Wrong, I Don't Wanna be Right," Millie Jackson

Monthly meeting of the Scarlet Letter Society.
Zoomdweebies Café
Friday, September 7, 2012
5:30 a.m.

Yes, we're reading a damn book this month. It's **Wifey** *by Judy Blume. You remember Judy Blume, from* **Are You There God, It's Me Margaret?** *Well, this was the slutty one after* **Forever** *and you weren't allowed to read either one of them growing up,* *so we're reading* **Wifey** *now. Pick up your copy from Zarina at Zoomdweebies ASAP.*

"The scarlet letter was her passport into regions where other women dared not tread."
-*The Scarlet Letter*, Nathaniel Hawthorne

Ron walked into her office with a raging boner. They had been sexting all morning, and he was horny as hell and couldn't take it another minute. He thanked the gods of pleasure that her office had blinds, and that they were normally kept shut. He was especially thankful for the lock on the door, one of the perks of having her name on it.

As he closed the door, he undid his tie. She looked up from her desk, above her dark teal cat-eye glasses, and smiled lazily.

"Looks like someone is glad to see me this morning."

"I can't stand it another minute," said Ron. "If you're going to be sending me pictures of your tits, this is what you should expect." He glanced down at his bulging crotch, where she was already looking.

She slowly unfastened the buttons of her mint green silk blouse. She wore a tight, short black skirt with a G-string underneath.

Removing her blouse revealed a skin-toned seamless lace bra that also allowed Ron a preview of her rosy nipples. They were already hardening in anticipation of his touch.

She placed the blouse over the edge of her cream leather office chair. She walked around to the front of her antique oak desk. She'd salvaged it from an auction for a ridiculous fifty dollars, and had learned in the past to be thankful for its sturdiness. She turned around to face away from Ron, who already had his hands on the sides of her ribcage as she swirled her hips and rubbed against him. He breathed out audibly. She cleared a few items from the desk and turned to face him. Removing her panties quickly, she placed her hands on the edge of the desk and hopped up. She already knew the angle was perfect.

Ron grabbed the back of her head with his left hand while his right hand explored and teased her nipples. She lifted her chest to meet his touch, reaching down to unbuckle his belt. His shirt was already on the floor from where he dropped it on the way to her desk, but his tie remained loosely around his neck. As he stepped out of his pants, she grabbed the tie to pull him back to her, passionately kissing him and darting her tongue into his eager mouth.

There wasn't much time for foreplay in an office where they knew anyone could come to the door. The heat of the encounter left little need for foreplay anyway. She held the tie with her left hand, using her right hand to stroke him a few times. He moaned softly.

"I want you," he said.

"Then take me," she responded, spreading her legs. She still wore one of the Jimmy Choo black leather pumps she'd put on that morning; the other had hit the floor when she jumped onto her own desk.

He thrust into her as she sighed, already wet from the sight of him walking through the door. She tightened her grip on the tie around his neck, twisting it tighter. He looked at her and raised an eyebrow.

"Oh that's how it's going to be?" he breathed.

"If I had time, you know I'd use it to tie you up," she said.

"I'd love it," he said. Sex between them was always a power play, and the exchange of that power was madly erotic to both of them. With his left hand around her ass, he used his right hand to grab her long, straight blonde hair and twist, then pull it firmly.

They came together in the frenzy of heat that only forbidden sex can generate. He looked into her ice blue eyes.

"That was amazing, Nicole," he said.

"It always is with us, Ron," she said. "Why don't we just get fucking married and call it a day?"

She winked at him and smiled a cocky smile, and he couldn't tell if she was serious or not. He found himself surprised at wishing that she was.

"Well maybe we should just think about doing something fucking insane like that one day," said Ron in what he hoped was the same are-we-kidding-or-not tone. He smiled at her as he got dressed. She walked around to the chair, put on her blouse as he put on his shirt, and they stared at each other while each buttoned buttons.

She walked around the desk, straightening the nameplate that read "Nicole Shaw, Managing Editor." At twenty-nine, she was the youngest woman in the history of the *Washington News* to serve this role, and she was quite pleased about it. Ron embraced her. They agreed to meet for cocktails after work, and he left the newspaper office and walked the two blocks to the law firm and his internship.

On the night of the Pop Rocks encounter, Eva had barely remembered returning to her room. The combination of the wine and the champagne and the romantic evening hit her all at once, and she wasn't even sure how she had made it into bed after the delicious night.

In the morning, she awoke in her bed and found a note.

Eva,

Seeing you vulnerable and taking care of you brought me many feelings. I want us both to take the day off today and enjoy the city and talk. Call me.

Charles

G-Chat With Charles
embradley@smithcohenbradley.com

9:35 PM **Charles**: *Madame, I owe you an apology.*

Eva: *Whatever for, darling chef?*

Charles: *We have been too distant. I feel it is my fault. It is not what I want, and I'm sorry.*

Eva: *You haven't done anything wrong. You were right. You had to physically carry me up to bed because I'd had so much to drink, so I was vulnerable. I know you had reasons for not wanting to worry about me.*

9:39 PM **Charles**: *You should not have to suffer because of what I went through losing my wife.*

Eva: *I didn't blame you. I've just been busy in DC- I'm sorry I haven't been to New York in a few weeks.*

9:40 PM **Charles**: *I wanted the evening to be perfect for you. Maybe the popping candy rocks were a bad idea?*

9:41 PM **Eva**: *I am spelling out "laughing out loud" right now because I don't think you would know what the LOL abbreviation would stand for. Pop Rocks. They are called Pop Rocks. And they were a perfectly wonderful idea.*

9:43 PM **Charles**: *If I am to be honest, I'm not sure how to handle my feelings for you.*

9:45 PM **Eva**: *I am always happy when I'm with you. You make me laugh. I can't thank you enough for that.*

Charles: *You fill my heart with joy.*

9:46 PM **Eva**: *That is probably the sweetest thing anyone has ever said to me — thank you.*

Charles: *I am scared to give you my heart because I cannot stand for it to be broken again.*

9:47 PM **Eva**: *I understand. But you should know I'm not an alcoholic like my father was. I know how to control my drinking. I know you didn't mean to suggest otherwise and be hurtful.*

Charles: *And for this I am so sorry to have even possibly hurt you, but not sorry to have cared.*

9:50 PM **Eva**: *Thank you for saying so. I'm sorry you're dealing with such a complicated woman. You deserve better, someone who would give you 100% of herself.*

9:51 PM **Charles**: *There is no better.*

Eva: *Let's talk about it when I get to New York. Maybe you can make the banana French toast you know I love.*

9:53 PM **Charles**: *Mais oui. Anything for our hotel's most distinguished guests, madame.*

Eva: *Well I have come to expect a certain level of treatment, thanks to your generous service, monsieur. I'll see you in a few days, Charles.*

9:55 PM **Charles**: *May time pass quickly until then.*

JUST A baby, wrote Lisa in her journal. *Only this.*

She looked at the words, and thought about it for a moment.

Was that really all she wanted?

It didn't seem to be that simple. If the only important thing in her life was having a baby, she'd be focused on making her marriage better, including having more sex as part of it, scheduling fertility treatments, resting, *whatever.* Not getting up at 3 AM and not being able to fall back asleep because she wondered if there was a new email from Ben.

What if? she wrote, *That Heart song could happen.*

She had thought of the song a hundred times lately, and now jotted down the song title: *"All I Want to Do Is Make Love to You."* The story in the song was that a woman's husband couldn't get her pregnant, so she trolled around picking up hot hitchhikers and taking them to a hotel room to have sex with them so that she could get knocked up. It worked, as proven by the lyric about running into the hitchhiker later on, while with her child. Lisa wrote down the remembered lyric: *"You can imagine his surprise, when he saw his own eyes."*

What a ridiculous song, thought Lisa, smiling almost to laughter. How many ways are there to get sperm in this world that a chick has to resort to driving around, picking up potential serial killer/STD carrying strangers, in order to get pregnant?

But what if it wasn't a stranger? she wrote. *What if it was a guy you knew, a guy whose child you wouldn't mind raising, even if he never knew of the child's existence?*

She wasn't even sure it was her husband's fault they couldn't get pregnant. He had been clocked with a low sperm count, but she knew that if they optimized all the conditions, she really should eventually be able to conceive in one of the months after years of trying. They really hadn't discussed it all that much. She never got the sense that having a baby was a priority for Jim, at least not like it was for her.

We're not even really trying that hard, Lisa wrote.

She thought of how Jim never really made it a priority. It wasn't like he was checking the calendar in the kitchen with the big red star on it every month, the date of her highest fertility. How she'd love it if he did something romantic on that date instead of bringing home a new pair of shoes for her that she didn't even want.

At least bring me some damn shoes on a red star day, wrote Lisa.

She resented the fact that he didn't care enough about how much she wanted a baby. And sometimes, deep in a part of her that no one would recognize, she fantasized about driving a Christian Louboutin spike heel right through his eyeball.

AT HER penthouse apartment overlooking the creek in downtown Keytown, Kate brought Maggie's tea to the coffee table. She had just returned from teaching her class at the liberal arts college and was happy to unwind. Maggie smiled, thanking her for remembering that Orange Pekoe with honey was her favorite.

They sat beside each other on the plush suede couch, enjoying the view and chatting. Maggie told Kate of her confusion over her relationship with Dave in light of her relationship with Ted, and how all of it was ridiculous in light of her divorce proceedings.

Kate listened. She reassured Maggie that none of it was out of the ordinary and that Maggie just seemed to be playing with boundaries and figuring out what she wanted in her life. Although Kate was once married, she had always identified herself as bisexual and shared an open marriage with her husband before he died.

Maggie asked her, "And what about this new relationship with you? It's been amazing, but as you know, I've never experienced anything like it. Now all of a sudden, I'm trying to figure out if I'm a lesbian, or what's going on."

Kate smiled at her. "Well, being with a woman for the first time in your late forties doesn't automatically mean you're a lesbian, although many women come out in their fifties. Besides, labels are always the things that cause all the problems for everyone. If only we could all learn to avoid them."

"You're right. The experience was just so completely unexpected," said Maggie. "And so completely natural. Being with a woman is night and day from being with a man, that's for sure."

"Oh no doubt," said Kate, smiling. "It's like having a girlfriend, but closer and obviously more intimate. It's like having the secret best friend you always wanted."

Maggie agreed. "Exactly. I mean, there we were, and you were so open about being bisexual and then me with my big mouth, asking you what it's like to be with a woman, because I was dating a guy who wanted a threesome with a girl, and I had never done that, and the next thing you know…"

"Yeah, the next thing you know we're completely naked in the stairwell of the town parking deck," said Kate, laughing.

"How did that even happen?" said Maggie.

"It's a good question," said Kate. "Clearly, since we have homes with bedrooms and beds, we could have chosen a more comfortable location. It was just the heat of the moment. The roof of the parking deck is so gorgeous with the view of the church spires and we had chatted for like two hours after that play was over. The moon…"

"I blame the moon," said Maggie.

"It's always the moon's fault," said Kate. She put down her tea and slid closer to Maggie on the couch. Maggie took a sip of her tea, smiled mischievously at Kate, and put down her tea as well.

"This setting is a little more comfortable, with the same great view of downtown," said Kate. She reached up and placed her hand on Maggie's curly hair, taking a single curl and twisting it gently between her fingers. Her dark blue eyes stared intently into Maggie's green ones.

"It is a great view," said Maggie, grinning as her eyes swept down across the cleavage of Kate's v-neck pink t-shirt. It was Sunday, Maggie had just closed her shop, and they were both in late summer garb of capri pants and t-shirts.

"So how are things with the Scarlet Letter Society?" asked Kate.

"Well, I love that we're reading books now," said Maggie. "Or at least pretending to."

"As your friendly neighborhood literature professor," said Kate, "I love that you're reading books with the infidelity theme. What a great way to explore the issues you're facing together as women."

"I think it really helps to see how women have handled their, um, 'flings' across the years, in books, anyway," said Maggie.

"Well, it is certainly true that they haven't fared very well when they cheat on their husbands," said Kate, smiling.

"I know. The poor things. It's really the reason our club exists. I hate that there are women out there, holding onto all this shame and guilt, feeling like they're alone in wearing the symbolic red "A" shirt 24-7," said Maggie. "I actually wish I could somehow find new women to join the group, but that would be a pretty awkward Craigslist ad."

"I always see it this way: for an affair to take place, three people are involved. There's the spouse who is having the affair, because their needs are not being met at home, the spouse who is being cheated on, and the affair partner who was in the right place at the right time," said Kate. "Our society blames the cheater, often hates the cheater. The person being cheated on is the victim in our culture, and often the hero in literature. But I don't think the cheater is always the bad guy. They *can* be, but many times, let's face it, the cheater wouldn't have cheated if they'd been happy in the first place."

"Well, I obviously don't think the cheater is always the bad guy either," said Maggie, "especially since I have certainly found myself in both roles."

"American society is so puritanical when it comes to fidelity," said Kate. "We act like we're this bunch of Victorian churchgoers with only the highest moral values. But our media and advertising, Internet porn habits, sex clubs, you name it, everything points to the truth of what Americans can often basically be, which is pretty kinky."

"That we are," Maggie agreed. "That we most certainly are. It's like we're a bunch of nuns walking around nodding reverently to one another, but under our habits, we're wearing slutty lingerie, garters, and nipple clamps, with Ben-Wa balls in our hoo-has."

"You know, I think those nipple clamps would totally show through Sister Elizabeth Anne's habit," laughed Kate.

"Hey, before I forget to mention it, your lovely daughter has been most helpful in acquiring copies for us," said

Maggie, "and even likes reading the books herself."

"Zarina was always a reader," said Kate. "I mentioned our friendship to her. Are you worried she'll figure out we're having a fling?"

"A fling," laughed Maggie. "What a great word. Yeah, I gotta admit to thinking about it when I'm at Zoomdweebies. Great shop name by the way, 80s girl. I've talked to Eva and Lisa outside of meetings and I know they'll be sure not to mention anything incriminating in front of Zarina while we're there."

"You know, it wouldn't be that big of a deal if she found out," said Kate. "She knows I have been with women, and she's open about experimenting with her own sexuality. She likes that adorable Stanley, but she's isn't sure she wants to be in a committed relationship with a guy. She said she's been thinking about girls lately."

"Really?" said Maggie. "Huh! Well I guess that apple doesn't fall far from the tree."

Kate let her right hand leave Maggie's soft curls and trail gently down her neck. Maggie closed her eyes and took a deep breath. Kate's fingers swept across Maggie's clavicle.

"I love this spot," she said, touching the small, soft pocket between Maggie's clavicle and her neck.

"I know just the one," said Maggie, and she reached out her right hand to touch the exact spot on Kate's neck. Kate sighed softly. She leaned over and kissed the soft pool of flesh on Maggie, leaving the spot with a gentle lick. Maggie traced her hand across Kate's shoulder and down her arm. She felt the goosebumps form on Kate's arm.

Kate reached over and touched the two bottom edges of Maggie's worn, vintage REO Speedwagon concert shirt and raised an inquisitive eyebrow. Maggie smiled. Kate gently lifted the t-shirt over Maggie's head.

They had time. There wouldn't be the rush of a frenzied passion and fear of discovery in a public parking deck—as much fun as that had been. This time, they'd be able to really enjoy each other.

Kate looked down at Maggie's black lace bra. "Beautiful," she said.

"So are you," Maggie said.

Kate ran her fingers slowly down from Maggie's clavicles and across her breastbone. Her hands gently found their way across the peaks of Maggie's breasts, bringing both to attention. Maggie sighed in pleasure and reached behind her back to unhook and remove her bra.

"You, too," she said, motioning towards Kate's t-shirt.

"In a minute," said Kate, smiling, and she leaned down and brought her mouth to Maggie's newly exposed breasts. Maggie put both of her hands in Kate's long, dirty blonde hair, appreciating her soft hair.

Kate bit down gently, looking up at her for permission. Maggie moaned out loud and said, "That feels incredible."

Kate attended to Maggie until Maggie couldn't take it anymore. She reached over and grabbed at Kate's t-shirt, which Kate whipped off and tossed off the couch, revealing her seamless red bra.

"I love the color scarlet."

"I love the way you say "scah-let," said Kate.

Maggie leaned over and kissed Kate full on the mouth. *Kissing a woman*, she thought, *there's another thing that is completely unlike being with a man.* Their smooth, supple lips came together. Minutes went by where they did nothing but kiss, their hands exploring each other's hair, wrapped behind each other's necks. Maggie reached down and found Kate's bra strap, unhooked and removed it, realizing this was the first time she'd done this on another woman. There hadn't been time for this level of nudity back in the parking deck.

Kate wore a smaller cup, but her breasts were already fully engaged by the time Maggie's thumbs found them. Maggie gently circled her hands around Kate's nipples, then more firmly, sometimes stopping to squeeze them between her thumbs and her index fingers. Kate groaned.

"Let's just get naked," said Kate.

"Right on," said Maggie, laughing.

They did. Pants and panties were on the floor in a matter of seconds. Kate tossed her head in the direction of the bedroom. Maggie followed. They flopped onto the bed.

"You're beautiful," said Kate, gently running her hand down Maggie's back. Maggie shivered. Kate gently rolled Maggie over to her side, and they lay facing each other, on their sides, each appreciating the feminine silhouette of the other.

Maggie looked at her. She was amazed at how much less self-conscious she felt about her naked body in front of another woman versus a guy, she'd thought it would be the other way around. But somehow maybe women just naturally accepted each other more easily than they were even able to accept themselves.

"You are a very lovely woman as well, professor," said Maggie. She'd been nervous about the whole "what do you do with a girl" thing the first time they'd been together, but this time she knew not to be nervous. She'd let her instincts take over.

Kate brushed her fingers down Maggie's side, across her arm, down her waist and hips, and around to her rear, which she squeezed gently.

"Your curves are amazing," she said.

Maggie placed her hand on Kate's hip bone, tracing the valley there between her side and her tummy. Kate was thin and small in figure, but she had a shapely ass, which Maggie now ran her hand across.

"I'm completely jealous of your ass," said Maggie, smiling at Kate.

"You know, it's not a bad ass," said Kate. "I don't love all my features, but the ass has come in handy for filling out the jeans."

Maggie slid toward her for a better feel. Kate slowly dragged the palm of her hand across Maggie's chest, raising goosebumps on Maggie and eliciting a sigh of pleasure. They kissed again, gently at first, then more firmly, their tongues exploring each other's soft mouths. Kate let her hand travel down Maggie's middle and between her thighs. Ever gently, she circled her fingers around Maggie's center. Maggie gasped in pleasure.

Kate shifted her position on the bed, straddling Maggie on all fours, so that their mouths could explore one another.

Maggie said simply, "Mmmmm…"

ZARINA LOUNGED across the brown leather couch in Zoomdweebies. It was a luxury she didn't normally allow herself, but it was a slow day in the shop and no customers were in the store. Her head was on the huge orange suede pillow, her leg was draped over the top of the couch, and she figured if she heard the *ding-a-ling* of the bell above the door, she could sit up quickly and not look like a total slacker.

She lounged because she was enraptured by Judy Blume's *Wifey*. Her mom had bought her all of Judy Blume's books when she was younger. She devoured *Tales of a Fourth Grade Nothing* and *Tiger Eyes* and *Are You There God? It's Me, Margaret* like they were candy. Blume's conversational writing style always made her feel like someone was just sitting next to her telling a story, and she was a funny writer. Zarina had never made her way all the way up to the ranks of *Forever* ("THE SEX ONE!" middle school friends had proclaimed) and *Wifey*, but here she was. She vowed to go back and read *Forever* after finishing this one.

She wondered how the Scarlet Letter Society gals were going to like *Wifey*. It was written in 1978, five years after *Fear of Flying*, so you'd think it would be drenched with the same bra-burning feminist enthusiasm as Jong's book. And yet once again, here they were with the slut shaming. The bored New Jersey housewife/mom Sandy (who slept in a separate bed from her husband!) had an affair, and then she got a sexually transmitted disease and went back to her amazingly boring spouse.

What the fuck, Judy!?

At least, *what-the-fuck* was how she thought Maggie and Eva and Lisa would respond to it. How couldn't they? *It's no different than the nineteenth century shit where the "whores" die in shame. Jong gives us a strong woman who is going to demand that her sexual needs be met if she returns to her husband. Blume gives us...an STD?* It was a bummer, because Sandy was a cool cat up until she didn't choose herself...again.

She couldn't wait to hear what the girls had to say, or whichever ones read it, and wondered if she was becoming sort of an unofficial club member. But just as she thought this, a text message came in to her phone:

> **Joy**: *Hey there Z! What up?*
> **Zarina**: *Not much. How are things at your shop?*
> **Joy**: *Boring. Wanna hang out later?*

Zarina: *I'd love it. Dinner, movie, drag queen karaoke? What's it gonna be?*

Joy: *All of those things, hopefully at the same time.* Lol

Zarina had been trying to convince herself the new relationship was just girlfriends getting together. But the more she'd spent time with Joy, the less she could deny her girl crush, and she wondered to herself if there was something more.

She heard the *ding-a-ling* of the door and jumped up, straightening the books on the coffee table. When she heard Stanley's laugh at seeing her straighten up from the couch, she relaxed, putting away her phone (which struck her as odd because she hadn't texted anything inappropriate) and turning around to smile at him.

He walked over to her, and despite his hipster skinny jeans and ironic black leather 80s bomber jacket, she thought he looked adorable. He hugged her, she hugged him back. She loved how he hugged her when they saw each other. It was so intense, so tight, like if he let her go he'd drown. And he always hugged for a good long time, too. Stan would hug Zarina for five minutes. He'd say "mmm" under his breath while he did it, too, like this hug was the best thing that ever happened to him.

When they finally stopped hugging, Stanley looked at her and said, "We need to talk."

She thought to herself, *no fucking way would he break up with me after that amazing hug.*

"Or," he said, seeing her concerned expression, "at least, I have something that I want to tell you."

And then he looked straight into her eyes, practically into her soul, and he said, "I fucking love you."

Zarina's expression turned to mystery at first, thinking he was being sarcastic or overly dramatic for some reason that hadn't yet been made apparent. And when she looked into his eyes, she saw he was serious.

"No," Stanley said. "I love you. I mean it. I'm tired of thinking it and being afraid to say it because you might not say it back, or because the time is not right. I know that I'm emotionally challenged or something and that I never tell you how I feel. But life is too short not to tell your favorite person in the world that you love them. And so I want you to know that I really do love you."

Despite her best efforts to stifle them, tears welled up in Zarina's eyes, simply because she didn't remember the last time someone had told her that in a romantic way. She couldn't believe how happy it made her to hear the words.

So she looked at her sweet boyfriend, feeling happy he was hers. "You're my favorite, too," she said. "And I love you right back."

And then they hugged again, even tighter than before.

LISA, MAGGIE and Eva sat around the table at Zoomdweebies on the first Friday of September, exchanging their usual banter and laughter and stories.

Zarina found herself hoping that someday when she was their age, she'd have a group of friends that she felt so "herself" around as these women did with each other.

Caramel lattes all around; she brought apple pie crumb cake to them, and they loved it.

"Well we missed you last month, *EVA!*" began Maggie with her traditional flair.

"I really missed you girls, too," said Eva. "I am so sorry I was unavoidably detained."

"What does that mean? Charles had to upgrade to a heavier chain gauge to hold you to the bed?" said Maggie.

Eva smiled, raised an eyebrow, and pursed her lips at Maggie.

"Well it wasn't exactly that kind of detainment, though I'd be up for it," Eva said. "Charles and I just decided to take the day off and enjoy the city together."

"Excuse me," said Lisa. "You decided to *what the what* off?"

"I know, I know," said Eva. "I'm not usually one to call in sick. But he made me this amazing dinner and put Pop Rocks in my vag for dessert, and then he asked me if I wanted to do like a New York touristy day, and we went to the Met and we did the whole carriage in Central Park thing, and then we went to see *Chicago* on Broadway. It was dreamy."

"Pardon me for just one moment," said Maggie. "I'm as big a fan of *Chicago* as anyone, but why are you talking about a Broadway musical when you just used the words "Pop Rocks" and "vag" in a sentence together? And did you also just use the word *'dreamy?'* What're you, Marcia-fuckin-Brady now? And horse carriage rides? Really? Tell me you weren't riding through Central Park with Pop Rocks in your vajayjay."

"It was surreal," Eva said, laughing. "I took a shower obviously, those things are sticky. And the horse ride was the next day. It was weird that we spent this day together — he never takes days off either," said Eva. "We just said screw it. Neither one of us is going to get fired, and God knows if either of us did, we'd probably breathe a sigh of relief. So we just decided to have fun."

"Fun," repeated Lisa.

"Yeah, what a concept, right?" said Eva. "It went by so fast. I think I hummed 'All That Jazz' half the way home on the train. I was sad it was over. Also, we had a little discussion about my wine drinking, but I convinced him I don't have a problem, I just like wine. The whole trip was just what I needed after the stress at home with Joe."

"Whoa, a smackdown with the French Chef? That's as new as the day off. What is going on with you two, and in a related matter, what are you going to do about your marriage?" asked Maggie. "Have you thought about it?"

"Oh well yes, I've thought about it a ton," said Eva. "And

I still don't know. It's not like I can leave the boys. And how am I supposed to tell Joe to leave his own house, right? So I made the decision, for now, to move into the spare bedroom. I am going to ask Joe for a separation, and if we work that out, we'll tell the boys."

"Why wouldn't you just ask him for a divorce?" asked Lisa.

"Well, ultimately that's what is going to happen, but in Maryland you have to be separated for a year before you can get a divorce unless you bring proof of adultery. It's like the 16th century. March the whore into the town square for the public stoning! So I'm just going to list my mom's place as a second address for now and do the pre-separation thing, I guess."

"And you haven't talked to Joe about any of this, not even that you know about what's-her-nurse?" said Maggie.

"I guess I'm going to need to do that this weekend," said Eva. "But not with the boys around. Maybe we'll go out for the most sad dinner ever. Ugh."

"That doesn't sound easy," said Lisa.

"No, it's going to be horrible," said Eva. "But I have a feeling I'll have a sense of freedom when I finally do it. And then as for Charles, it will be easier to see where that relationship could go while I'm not stuck under the dead weight of this one. But I have to say, some days I feel like swearing off relationships completely."

"It's just like Hawthorne says; 'she didn't know the

weight until she felt the freedom,'" said Maggie.

"Anyway, speaking of books? I didn't read the whole thing," admitted Eva. "Started it though."

"You might not even want to finish it," said Lisa. "I thought it was depressing. Blume's narration is as flawless as it always has been, but the story ends up being awful at the end."

"The main character Sandy is so close to having it all together," said Maggie. "She figures out what she wants, goes for it, then it all falls apart and she goes back to the husband that makes her miserable. Why would you do that?"

"Who knows?" said Lisa. "Why stay with someone who makes you unhappy?"

Eva looked at her.

"Who did you just ask that question?" she said to Lisa.

"Oh, well, we just learned you're not going to stay with someone who makes you unhappy anymore," said Lisa. "And as for me, it's not like I am completely unhappy... I'm just sort of not really happy. I need to figure out a way to do something about that somehow."

Maggie asked, "So if you're not happy and you're not unhappy, what are you?"

"Married?" said Lisa.

And they all laughed.

October 2012

"Are you gonna stay with the one who loves you? Or are
you going back to the one you love?"
- "The One You Love," Glenn Frye

Monthly meeting of the Scarlet Letter Society.
Zoomdweebies Café
Friday, October 5, 2012
5:30 a.m.

*Zarina has copies of Madame Bovary at Zoomdweebies. Don't
blow it off just because it's historical fiction, EVA.*

"The scarlet letter was her passport into regions where
other women dared not tread."
-*The Scarlet Letter*, Nathaniel Hawthorne

Lisa opened the email at her laptop in the kitchen of her house in the subdivision in which she hated to live. She didn't understand why they couldn't be in one of the gorgeous brownstones downtown near her business, but her ever-practical husband Jim had insisted the property value would be better here. Since the real estate market had crashed, Lisa doubted it. The building where she rented her bakery was for sale, and Lisa had been trying to figure out a way to convince Jim that she should buy the downtown building. They could convert the two upstairs apartments into a two-level home that would be big enough for the two of them and even for the baby she yearned for.

She'd pick up her copy of *Madame Bovary* from Zarina, but this book club aspect of the SLS was getting disheartening. Here she was, trying to find a way to justify potentially having an affair with her graphic designer, and all the literature pointed towards adulterous women ending up dead, otherwise humiliated, or contracting sexually transmitted diseases.

And now that she had learned about Ben's son, she wondered what it meant for their potential affair. *Is it really even a potential affair? How much of the mutual attraction is just in my head?* Every nerve ending in her body was alive when she was with Ben, and she couldn't believe the feeling wasn't mutual. She felt like he was attracted to her. They met, and her whole body screamed "JUST KISS ME!"

The thought scared the complete hell out of her. *What if*

he did kiss me? She knew they'd end up sleeping together.
Was that truly what she wanted? She thought so, but she
wasn't positive.

She tried to think about consequences and outcomes of
an affair, but it was hard to think with her brain when her
heart and her body were just telling her to go for it.

And it was at that moment, with Lisa deep in thought,
staring blankly at the October SLS invite in front of her, that
her husband walked into the kitchen.

"You look like you're really concentrating on something,"
said Jim. "What is it?"

Lisa looked at him. "Oh, it's nothing," she answered,
composing herself. "I was just going over the bakery orders
for the day. I need to get into town soon and fire up the oven."

"Can we talk for a few minutes?" Jim asked as he walked
over to pour himself a cup of coffee.

"What is it?" said Lisa, concerned at his tone.

"I just thought we should sit down and chat about a few
things. We're always just rushing around. I feel like you've
been kind of stressed lately. This is kind of awkward to bring
up, but I know that my — um, preferences about feet annoy
you," said Jim. "I'm ashamed of it. I really do try my best
not to act on my fantasies that often, but the last thing I want
to do is be a turnoff to my wife while we're trying to have a
baby."

"Thank you for saying that," said Lisa, pleased he was
even mentioning trying to conceive. "I don't think you

should be ashamed of it," said Lisa. "I knew about your foot fetish when we started dating years ago. At first, it was a lot of fun…"

"Yeah, and now it's something that is coming between us and that is not what I want," said Jim.

"Well, it isn't as much about the sexual part of it as the expense," said Lisa. "There are many more things I'd like to do with money than spend it on expensive shoes that I can't wear to the bakery."

"I'm sorry," said Jim. "That's why I wanted to talk. I just want you to know that I started seeing a therapist in DC to talk about my fetish, and I am working on it. And also, I signed up for some more tests to try to get more information about any fertility issues I might have. I know you're always working on it and thinking about it," he gestured toward the calendar, "and I want to feel like I have a part in trying to make our family happen."

"Wow," said Lisa. "Thank you. It's really nice of you do that for me."

"I honestly just really want you to be happy," said Jim.

"I want both of us to be happy, too," said Lisa. "I'm so thankful you decided to bring this up and I appreciate your honesty."

She walked across to the coffeemaker and kissed her husband. Maybe, for once, they could have unscheduled sex…while she was barefoot.

EVA WAS sitting at her desk in New York City, working on a case that was scheduled to go to trial the following week, when the call came.

"Eva? It's Marvin Schubert on Matthews Island." Marv was the next door neighbor of her mother. He lived in the cottage beside hers near the waterfront. He had never called her before, and she couldn't imagine how he had gotten her number.

Eva was immediately concerned. "Hi, Marv..." she began.

"I am so very sorry to have to be the one to deliver this news. There's been a car accident. Your mother..."

"My mother?" repeated Eva. Her entire body froze.

"I'm afraid she didn't make it," said Marv.

"Didn't make it?" She heard the words coming out of her mouth, repeating him like a parrot, but she didn't know what she was saying. She couldn't get her brain around the concept that anything could happen to her mom. She had just left her days before; Mom had waved to her from the front yard of her cottage, like she always did when Eva left. She was *there*. She was always there.

"The accident happened not far from the drawbridge. It wasn't her fault. A deer ran across the road and she swerved to avoid it... Since I'm a fire company volunteer, I was there to respond to the call from another motorist. She's been taken to the hospital, but she was pronounced dead at the scene. Someone more official will call you, I'm sure, but I thought..."

"When did it happen? Which way was she traveling? Was she conscious when you got to the scene?" Questions streamed out of Eva as her head spun.

"It was just a few hours ago," responded Marv. "One of her neighbors said she was headed to her knitting club meeting in St. Luke's. She died on impact, so she did not suffer. If there is anything else I can..."

"No, thank you for calling, Marv. I'll be on the next plane to Maryland," said Eva, and she hung up.

Her body remained completely still, and her eyes shifted to the photos on her desk. There was a photo of her two smiling boys in their lacrosse uniforms one day after a game they'd won, and there was a photo of her mother, sitting in her Adirondack chair in front of the cottage, facing the water. She had her reading glasses on, and you could see newspapers on the ground in front of her. She was smiling up at Eva. The photo was her favorite because it was impromptu and casual.

The photo of her mother triggered a memory for Eva. Her father, coming in late usual, drunk as always. Her mother tried so hard for so long to pretend everything was ok: put a happy face on, and some makeup, and pretend the bad part is not happening. *Just a normal family, nothing to see here, move along.* Like any codependent person, Joan Bradley had been in complete denial of her husband's drinking problem. She preferred to live in a world of illusion; smoke and mirrors, because who wanted to see the reality as it truly was? Certainly not her.

Eva pictured her mother at the kitchen stove, cooking a roasted chicken dinner, actually wearing an apron and asking *how was your day, Eva?* even as they could hear her drunken husband stumbling his way through the house, angrily asking if dinner was ready. The stench of stale beer filled her mind and her office. Eva hated beer to this day. She had never seen her father drink a glass of wine or champagne, so somehow, she thought her own drinks of choice meant she was different enough from him. She shook her head and the tears came.

She hadn't thought about it until now, but as she looked at the photos on her desk, she realized that her husband wasn't in any of them. Yet she was an only child, so it was her husband she called first, dialing his private cell line that was separate from his work number; the number was basically reserved for family emergencies. *Your emergency contact*, she thought. That's the person you call when there is an emergency. Even if you couldn't remember the last time you had dialed their number. Joe answered immediately.

"My mother," Eva began. It took her a moment to even form the words. "Is dead. She died. In a car accident."

"Oh, God. I am so sorry, Eva," said Joe. "What happened? When?"

"She hit a deer on her way to her knitting class a few hours ago," answered Eva, tears running down her face.

"She didn't suffer. I am taking the next flight home in two hours."

"Are you ok to travel?" Joe asked.

"I guess so," she said.

"Let me know what time your plane lands and I'll pick you up from the airport. Call me when you land. I will speak with the boys."

"Thank you," said Eva, and she hung up the phone. And then she screamed, not loudly, but an aching, choked sound, before collapsing onto her desk in wrenching sobs.

MAGGIE PLACED the phone receiver down, devastated at her friend's news, just as Ted walked into her shop. They had plans to go see *Cabaret*, which was playing at the historic downtown theatre Wes managed. It was "vintage movie night." Ted looked handsome as always. She felt badly going out for a night on the town while Eva was in such a bad place, but Eva had told her they'd get together the next day when Eva was back home.

"What's wrong?" said Ted. Even though she hadn't said anything, Ted could see the concern etched on Maggie's face.

"I just got some really sad news about Eva's mother," Maggie said. "She was in a car accident and died." Maggie thought for a moment about how to this day she didn't know if her own mother was alive or dead.

She had just left a lunch with Dave, and she was feeling

conflicted; a feeling she was growing weary of. She couldn't understand why she seemed to need so much attention from men (make that "people," she thought), and it irked her. *Do I really need to have multiple dates with my ex-husband and my lover (um, one of them) in the same day?*

Maggie put down her copy of *Madame Bovary*. "And also, I was just reading our Scarlet Letter Society book club book, and I have a feeling things are going to go badly for the heroine somehow."

"I've never read it, so I couldn't tell you," said Ted. "But historically, women adulteresses don't do very well, do they?"

"Not a bit," said Maggie. "'Punish the Whore' is a true literary theme for the ages."

Maggie picked up her laptop to order flowers to send to Eva's house. She thought about the irony of how annoyed she had been getting at the female characters in these books, when she wasn't liking her own choices much better. She could only hope that like Isadora Wing, she'd burn through a bunch of madness and finally work it all out at the end. She sure as shit didn't want the Karenina kill or the Wifey wimp-out for her own ending.

She realized how ridiculous it was that she felt lonely much of the time. Between her two ex-husbands (though technically she didn't ever see the most recent ex), her two current lovers and some great girlfriends, she really should have no reason to feel lonely. But the fact of the matter was that most mornings she woke up alone. And for some reason, though going to bed could be lonely, especially if you woke up for some reason in the middle of the night, waking up and drinking coffee or eating breakfast alone was absolutely the loneliest thing in the world.

There was no lonely worse than *coffee lonely*.

"So how are things with your band?" she asked, changing the subject intentionally.

"Really good," said Ted. "I may have to quit my day job!"

"For real?" said Maggie, genuinely happy. "That would be great." She loved going out to listen to the band play, and the venues around Baltimore and DC had gotten bigger and bigger. She knew the band's following had grown online and that Ted was exhausted trying to maintain a "real" 9 to 5 job in addition to writing music and singing for the band.

"Yeah, we're heading down to Nashville for a week actually to play a few gigs and meet with a record producer there," said Ted. "Not bad for a bunch of middle age guys everyone expects would be hanging out in local bars playing Jimmy Buffet cover songs by now."

"Good for you, Ted," said Maggie. "I'm really happy for you." She walked over, hugged her handsome lover, and felt a pang of sadness. How much longer would this affair last? She knew he was seeing other women, though it wasn't something they ever discussed, it was something she suspected. She hadn't asked because she hadn't wanted to know the answer.

"So are we ready to go watch Liza Minnelli do some jazz hands?" said Ted. She kissed him, squeezing his hand.

"Hell yeah," she said. "Let's go watch some vintage Broadway history while we make out in the back of the theatre."

He laughed, and they held hands as they walked through the town together.

At the historic Patrick Theatre, Wes greeted them in the lobby.

"Well look what the cat dragged in," he said.

"Nice to see you, too, Wesley," said Maggie.

"Hello, there, Ted," said Wes. "Didn't know you were a Liza fan."

"I'm a fan of anything playing here," said Ted, "and as a musician it's mandatory I have an appreciation for Judy Garland's daughter."

Ted and Maggie walked over to the bar and bought cocktails and candy: a pair of Caramellos.

"These are such a random candy to have," said Maggie to Wes as she sipped her rum and Coke. "I love Caramellos. And you have Whatchamacallits and Zero bars, too. All my favorites."

"We try to do a vintage candy thing to match the history of the theatre," said Wes. "There are all kinds of candies through the ages." He pointed out the display showing the decades: penny candy from the 20s all the way through the 90s and the 00s.

"This is such a great idea," said Ted.

"Well, everyone gets sick of Sno-caps and M&Ms at regular movie theatres," said Wes. "Though we do carry those, it's fun to pick out candies from the vintage candy companies online. Can't say I hate the candy buying part of my job."

"I'm going to run to the ladies' room," said Maggie, finishing her drink. "I'll meet you inside in a sec."

"Alright," said Ted. "I'll pick out great seats."

And as Maggie walked back out of the ladies' room, she saw a couple standing at the candy counter, where she had been just moments before. She'd recognize that longish curly hair and that flannel shirt a mile away, with the dressier jeans, not the ones with holes in them. It was Dave. And he was with an absolutely gorgeous woman about ten years younger than they were.

She should have ignored them, simply walked by and gone to her seat. But she didn't. Something took over her common sense, and she marched right up to the unsuspecting couple, feeling like a complete hypocrite since her own lover was right inside the theatre.

"Hi Dave," said Maggie in what she hoped was a genuine-sounding, neutral voice.

Dave looked a bit surprised, but her smiled at her warmly.

"Hello, Margaret," he responded. Maggie looked at the younger woman. Her caramel-colored hair was in perfect blown-out curls, her makeup flawless, her black dress clinging in all the right places.

"Hi, I'm Maggie," she boldly addressed her. "I'm Dave's wife. Well, first wife. Nicer than the second wife, I'd argue." Dave looked simultaneously annoyed and horrified. "It's funny, from the back I would have thought you were one of our daughters."

Dave cleared his throat (which Maggie recognized as essentially saying *Fuck You* under his breath.)

"Margaret, this is Callie. She works at the national preservation office in PR."

"Oh, a building saver," said Maggie.

Callie looked at Maggie evenly and coolly, with a slight hint of condescension that made Maggie want to kick her in the shin, like she would've done to the bully on the blacktop playground 30 years ago.

"We do what we can," she said,. "Nice to meet you Margaret." And then she turned her back, as if selecting candies whose brands were older than she was more interesting than this conversation.

Maggie glared at Dave. "You two have a good evening!" she said, in the most even tone she could muster. She stormed toward the theatre, willing away the tears in her eyes.

How ridiculous! She thought. *What the goddamn hell am I crying about? Of course he has some slutty gorgeous girlfriend. Why wouldn't he? We aren't together. He knows I have two lovers. One of them is right here in this building.*

So she pulled herself together and walked into the theatre

just as *Cabaret's* opening strains of "Willkomen" began to play.

Eva walked out from the baggage area into the rainy, breezy air at Baltimore Washington International Airport. Just as she exited the sliding glass doors, she saw Joe's Hummer pull up to the curb. She was thankful not to have to wait in the cold. He got out of the car, hugged her a bit stiffly, saying, "I'm so sorry," then put her suitcase in the back.

She got into the car.

"I don't know how to do funeral arrangements," she said blankly. "And I've never hated being an only child as much as I do right now. There's no one to call to help me."

"I'll help you get through this, Eva," said Joe matter-of-factly. His medical precision and attention to detail were going to be a huge benefit to her over the next few miserable days. "I called the hospital where your mother was taken and contacted the funeral home. You just have a lot of decisions to make about a service, cemetery, obituaries, those kinds of things."

"I don't know how I can make any of those decisions," said Eva. "I still can't believe Mom is gone. It still feels like the next time I drive to the island, she'll come out the door of the cottage to greet me."

"You're still in denial," said Joe. "It's the first step in the grieving process, and you're going to be experiencing many different emotions in the coming weeks."

She realized he had given this speech to countless patients' families over the years, only the horror of discussing death with the parents of a dying young child was unimaginable to her. She still didn't appreciate his clinical tone in such an emotional set of circumstances, but she had grown to expect it. She didn't want to talk about her mother anymore.

"Do you love her?" Eva said, and she turned to face her husband.

"*What*?" said Joe. "What the hell are you talking about, Eva?"

"I know you're seeing someone," she said.

"You know what, Eva, there is a time and a place for everything," said Joe, "and if you want to sit down and have a discussion our marriage and our future, we can do that, but I do not think that right now is a good time for that conversation. You have enough to deal with."

"So you do love her," said Eva, absently. She looked out the window and began to cry. She was so sick of crying, and as a normally strong woman she absolutely *hated* crying in front of people, yet crying seemed like all she ever did lately.

"I didn't say that," said Joe. "I simply said I don't think now is a good time to be discussing relationships given your state of crisis."

"I think now is a perfect time," said Eva. "If my life is going to fall apart, it may as well fall all the way apart. I know you're seeing someone."

"Are you going to pretend you aren't seeing anyone?" said Joe. "I guess if you want to do this now, we can do it, but I still don't think it's a good idea."

"You and I haven't had sex in so many months I can't even remember the last time," said Eva. "I am not sure where our marriage train ran off the tracks, but it hasn't been viable for a long time."

"I know," said Joe. "I have thought about it for awhile and I know I am partly to blame. I'm sorry. My career took over my life for so many years."

"You definitely chose career over family," said Eva. "I practically raised those boys alone while trying to advance my own career, which is equally as important as yours. The au pair spent more time with your sons than you did."

"Look, Eva, it's hard enough for me to say I'm sorry for anything when you know those are words I am not used to," said Joe. "I have done the best I could to be a provider for this family, even if it meant working ridiculous hours over the years to try to provide the fine home and lifestyle we all enjoy."

"I was working very hard too, Joe," said Eva, annoyed that he was giving a martyr speech when she had carried the weight of both a full time career and motherhood.

"I'm sorry," said Joe. "I am trying my best to be open here. I don't know if it helps for you to hear it, but I am. We just grew apart, we became different people, and I should've done something to fix that."

And in that moment, where Joe used the words "I'm sorry" a second time, words she knew he never, ever said, she momentarily remembered why she had fallen in love with him those years ago. His vulnerability, so carefully tucked away behind his years of medical training and jaded years of losing patients, was one of the things that once drew her to him. *So strong on the outside, so emotionally fragile in many ways on the inside.* Like everyone, he struggled with his own past demons. Regardless of the hurt and anger and sorrow of the present, she felt a profound sadness for the loss of the past.

"You spend your entire days trying to fix people," said Eva. "And I don't blame you for letting our marriage fail. I let it fall apart, too. When I didn't have my needs met by you, I found other ways to have them met. I should've thrown a flag years ago when I knew I was miserable. But when you're raising kids and trying to manage a career, sometimes your marriage just takes a backseat. It's sad."

"It is sad," said Joe.

"When all of this is over with my mother, I want a divorce," said Eva. "Our marriage is too broken to fix, and neither one of us would even know how. But I don't want it to be ugly and awful and I don't care about money and things and if there is any way to have it somehow be peaceful, then that is what I want for us."

"Ok," said Joe. "I do not want to fight with you. We can talk more about all this when things settle down, but Eva I don't want this to be ugly either. We have the boys to think about."

"I just want to get home and hug my boys," said Eva.

"You know they love you," said Joe. "I probably never said it, but you have always been a good mother to them."

Eva swallowed, looked out the window where the rain fell softly, and now that she was home, she finally let the tears flow freely for the loss of her mother.

ZARINA SWEPT the floor. The coffee couldn't brew fast enough when it was dark outside on a cold fall morning. Maryland autumns were the strangest: one day it could be raining and miserable and 42 degrees, and the next day it could be sunny and 70. "Dress in layers," her mom used to say. And to this day, she did. Short sleeved t-shirt, hooded zipper jacket, and a warmer, waterproof jacket on a hook somewhere nearby.

The smell of pumpkin cheesecake muffins baking filled the air of the shop. Zarina knew the SLS girls would eat the hell out of those, and so would Stanley. Her mom's recipe was a pain in the ass to make but every bit worth it. And the crumb topping? To die for.

"Good morning, Zarina," said Lisa as she walked into the shop, shuddering her shoulders against the chill. The fake fireplace heater was cheesy-looking, but it worked well enough to warm the couch area. Lisa scurried over to it right away, warming her hands by the "fire."

"Hi, Lisa," Zarina greeted her. "Good to see you. How're

things?"

"Oh, busy," she said, but a frown lingered at the edges of her mouth. "I don't know if you heard, but Eva's mom died."

"Oh. Oh my God, that is so awful. Poor Eva!" said Zarina.

"I know, I feel so badly for her," Lisa answered. "Especially with Thanksgiving and Christmas around the corner."

Zarina walked over to the shop door to open it for Maggie and Eva, giving Eva a huge hug and telling her how sorry she was.

"Welcome, ladies," Zarina said. "Pumpkin cheesecake muffins coming up in a few minutes. Let me know what kind of coffees you'd all like today."

"Thanks, Zarina," said Eva.

"I'm just glad we're all able to be together," said Maggie, and the ladies took their usual places in the cozy brown leather couch area, settling in.

Zarina had a feeling October would mean pumpkin lattes, so she set about making their coffee orders while they began their gathering.

Lisa walked over to where Eva was sitting and hugged her.

"I'm so sorry," she told Eva.

"The memorial service was really lovely, Eva," said Maggie.

"Joe really helped me out with all of that," said Eva. "And my mom's neighbor Marv helped me with all the details of the burial and the reception at the house on the island."

Eva paused for a moment. The mention of the burial flashing her back to the cemetery. As her mother's body was lowered into the ground next to her father's, all Eva could think about was *why would she want to buried next to that drunk asshole who did nothing but make her entire life miserable?* She shook off the memory along with the chill from outside.

"It had to be so hard to get through all of that," said Lisa. "When my dad died, my mom was a mess. Even though he had cancer and we knew that it was coming, it didn't make it any easier when it happened. My brother and sister and I were devastated."

"I don't think you can ever be ready for something like death," said Eva. "I'm glad Mom didn't have to suffer in any way, because she had talked about being afraid of being in pain. If she had to choose a way to go, it would have been something like this, where at least she didn't have to suffer and I didn't have to see her in pain. She wouldn't have wanted that."

"I loved the way you had all the photos from over the years displayed at the house," said Maggie. "How did you get that all together?"

"Oh gosh, I just gathered the ones mom had kept around the house and some from boxes in the attic and got matching frames and put them together," said Eva. "It was actually nice to have some busy work to do during those days."

"You will always carry her with you," said Maggie. "She's part of who you are."

Maggie looked down for a minute as she thought about how mothers are always part of who we are, even the kind of mother who abandons you. *Do I carry that around? Abandonment? Leaving people so they can't leave me?*

"It's true," Zarina said, taking the liberty of interrupting the conversation only because she knew what it was like to lose a parent. "I'm so sorry, Eva."

She delivered lattes and muffins and then faded into the background again, not wanting to be a distraction to such an emotional scene between the women.

"You know, we should talk about the book," said Eva. "Because with everything I had going on and taking off work for the two weeks, I had time to sit around and actually read it."

"Oh, God," said Maggie. "More death. Are we sure we want to do that this month? We can skip it completely..."

"No, let's talk about it," said Eva. "I mean, all these women dying or getting STDs in these books just because they've had affairs seems kind of ridiculous, doesn't it? At least the one girl, Isadora, didn't die. That's been the best one so far. I did write down one quote from *Madame Bovary*, because it came at such an opportune time and it is so true: 'Death always brings with it a kind of stupefaction, so difficult is it for the human mind to realize and resign itself to the blank and utter nothingness.' It's the nothingness that's the hardest." Eva's eyes filled with tears.

"Even though there is death, Emma is so beautiful in

her tragedy," said Lisa. She took out her journal, the trusty, faded book in which she'd taken notes on each and every book they'd read. She read:

"Before she married, she thought she was in love; but the happiness that should have resulted from that love, somehow had not come. It seemed to her that she must have made a mistake, have misunderstood in some way or another. And Emma tried hard to discover what, precisely, it was in life that was denoted by the words 'joy, passion, intoxication', which had always looked so fine to her in books."

"It does always somehow seem better in books, doesn't it?" said Maggie. "except when you fucking die at the end of the book, then maybe not so much. I just don't get this whole 'you're in love, you don't play by the rules society expects of you, you die' storyline."

"So true," said Eva, sniffling. "Who wrote all these books? Catholic priests?"

"Sure seems like it," said Lisa. "Like we don't have enough guilt in our lives already without feeling like we're supposed to feel guilty because it's what the literature says."

"Well, I haven't had guilt about anything in a long time," said Eva. "I think you actually have to still love a person to feel guilty about cheating on them, and I haven't been in love with Joe for probably a decade. We have finally decided to get a separation and divorce."

"Oh, wow," said Maggie. "that is big news. You've had a tough month. Are you ok with it?"

"It feels like a relief," said Eva. "Like I'll be free. The marriage was a façade for so long. I didn't even realize how unhappy I was until I started finding happiness in other places. I can't say I'm not sad in some ways, and I definitely feel like a marriage failure, but it seems like it will be pretty peaceful."

"It takes two people to allow a marriage to fail," said Lisa. "But fail isn't even really a good word. It's an ending and another beginning. I am sure the divorce will be tough for the boys, but once they make it through, the peacefulness will be good for them and for you."

"I hope so," said Eva. "I know high school is a tough time, so I hope this doesn't make it worse for them, but I can't believe having two happy parents in different places isn't going to be better for them than having two miserable ones in the same place."

"That has got to be true," said Maggie.

"Enough about me," said Eva. "I want to know what is going on with you two. I haven't been around much to see you and catch up on the latest news in your love lives."

"My husband is in counseling for the foot fetish and some additional fertility testing, too," said Lisa, "and Ben is...well, he's just...Ben."

"No steamy stories of hot sex under covered bridges for us today, Lisa?" asked Maggie.

"Not today," said Lisa. "He came to the shop for lunch recently..."

"And then he helped you eat some pie?" said Eva.

"He loves my pie," said Lisa with a smirk.

"I'll bet he does," said Maggie. "Well girls, I have to report things are a little confusing for me lately. Too many people in my life. I want to simplify things, but I don't know how. I'm too old for all this action. I want to settle down. I just want someone who will be there to have coffee with every morning, maybe even bring it to me in bed once in awhile."

"That," said Eva, "absolutely has to be the truest love of all. Someone who will bring you coffee in bed."

"Absolutely," said Lisa. "I think that's all *Madame Bovary* ever wanted. She might have even made it to the end of the book if she had a guy bringing her coffee in bed."

November 2012

"Tempted by the fruit of another/Tempted but the truth
is discovered/What's been going on /Now that you have
gone /There's no other."

-"Tempted," Squeeze

Monthly meeting of the Scarlet Letter Society.
Zoomdweebies Café
Friday, November 2, 2012
5:30 a.m.

Pick up book of the month from Zarina: **The Awakening** *by*
Kate Chopin.

"The scarlet letter was her passport into regions where

other women dared not tread."
-*The Scarlet Letter*, Nathaniel Hawthorne

L isa sat at the counter of her shop with her coffee. The air was filled with the smell of holiday pumpkin and apple pies baking. Her laptop was in front of her. She'd just opened the SLS invite from Maggie. She had already read *The Awakening*, but would pick up her copy to give it a second look. *Oh Christ*, she thought, *we can't get away from whore-punishing death around here, can we?* She might skip the second reading and just find some quotes from Goodreads to bring to the meeting. She thought about telling Maggie that maybe they should read books about something else- *anything else-* for awhile.

She sat down and began to work on how to phrase the email she wanted to send to Ben. She wanted to see him again, but she didn't want to seem overeager.

from: **Lisa** lswain@blackbirdspie.com
to: **Ben** bnidale@starfishdesign.com

date: Thursday, November 1, 2012 at 9:10 AM

subject: Graphic

> I love my new logo so much that I
> ordered t-shirts. Made sure they weren't
> all girly colors, so I could save one
> for you to thank you for your perfect
> graphic design. Wanna grab a drink one
> day after work so I can bring your shirt?
> ☺ L

This was the third version of the email. *Should I ask to have lunch? Was asking to have drinks too forward? Why didn't he just make out with me when he was in my shop the last time?* She felt like a fool. It had been awhile since they'd even communicated. She didn't even know if he was as sexually interested in her as she was him, or if he was at all. The electricity between them seemed obvious to her, but maybe she was imagining it. There was no way in hell she was going to be making the first move physically, but she knew if he made it, she could not turn him down.

She hit send, and immediately the guilt, because she knew her husband was trying to patch things up between them. Ben answered her almost immediately.

from: **Ben** bnidale@starfishdesign.com
to: **Lisa** lswain@blackbirdspie.com

date: Thursday, November 1, 2012, 9:14 AM

subject: Booze and t-shirts

> Well if it isn't the lovely baker putting the booze invite out there. Hmmmm...I guess technically now that my firm's work for you is complete, you're not formally a client anymore. Therefore, engaging in drunken t-shirt exchanges seems entirely appropriate. Pick a day.

> Ben

Lisa smiled, feeling her cheeks flush. *That's right*, she thought. I guess the whole "professional" relationship was over now that her logo was on the window sign, t-shirts were here and the website was all but complete. So now what? This was the question she was going to have to answer for herself, especially before her lightweight ass hit the barstool next to her hunky "former graphic designer." She answered him with three words: *Why not today?* and hit send. And then she walked over and took the fresh, steaming apple pie from the oven.

ZARINA AND Stanley met at the restaurant simply because they could both walk there. Stanley had said he wanted to try the new fancy celebrity chef's restaurant on Commerce Street, and she'd been surprised. Usually he wasn't the type of guy who wanted to go fancy. Zarina had mentioned the restaurant a few weeks before, but maybe he had just seen the guy on t.v. and wanted to try it out. She was thrilled to get dressed up in something other than the usual t-shirt/ jeans attire. Heels! Makeup! Perfume! All rarities for her. But it was always fun to feel like a girly girl once in awhile.

She chose a peach colored velvet Juicy dress she'd found at an upscale consignment shop downtown. It looked nice with her caramel skin and black hair. Black tights and boots, and she cracked open last year's Sephora holiday box of makeup for one of the first times to pick out fun eye shadow shades and a lipstick. She stood in the lobby of the restaurant, which was a renovated historic brownstone mansion complete with curved terraces on the upper floors, bay windows, and beautiful stained glass.

Stanley walked in, and he was wearing a tie, and she laughed, not meaning to, but she couldn't help it. He just looked so awkward in the thing. Zarina felt bad about laughing so she shuffled over and hugged him.

"You're laughing because I'm wearing a tie," he said.

"It looks fantastic. I'm sorry. I just don't know if I've ever seen you in one."

"You know," he smiled at her, "I could say something about how that was probably the first time I've hugged you at this new higher height since I don't think I've ever seen you in heels before."

"You are correct, sir," she said. "I bet you haven't seen

me in heels before."

"And what is that stuff on your eyes?" he said, faking bewilderment.

"Ha ha, ok, very funny, let's go act like we belong in this fancy schmancy place before we both turn back into pumpkins," she said, and they entered the restaurant.

"Mr. and Mrs. Dean?" the bow-tied butler type walked over and asked.

"I'm Stanley Dean," said Stan, "and this is... Zarina."

She covered her mouth to hide a laugh at his formal tone of voice, because she did not want to look like a jackass and make a scene in what felt like a high society kind of place.

They sat down at a table between the beautiful picture window facing the street and the marble fireplace. She looked across at him in his slightly wrinkled soft blue corduroy shirt and plaid flannel tie. Only Stanley would wear a plaid flannel tie. She smiled at him.

"See? We CAN have nice things," he said, returning her smile.

"Now there's nothing wrong with eating Chinese food out of boxes in front of *Fast Times at Ridgemont High*," Zarina said.

"Not at all," he said. "But once in awhile it is nice to dress up in real people clothes."

"Yes, real people clothes are ok once in awhile," she agreed. They talked in the natural way they always did. He was graduating in the spring, and she'd just started taking grad classes, and they were both ready for Christmas break already.

The pair enjoyed a delicious meal. Oyster stew and blue cheese wedge salads and pan seared scallops and they shared the chocolate banana bread pudding for dessert. Zarina was stuffed.

"It looks like your carriage has arrived, princess," he said, gesturing towards the window.

She looked out to see a quaint horse drawn carriage. What was this? She looked inquiringly at Stan, thinking maybe he was joking.

"I got tickets to the orchestra at the arts center," said Stan. "And it looks like our ride is here."

She was amazed. "What did I do to deserve all this?" she asked. "Or what did you do wrong that you haven't told me?"

"I just thought it was time for a night where you felt like royalty," he said. "You work really hard and you deserve it."

"Wow," she said. "Well then I guess I'll take it."

They walked out into the chilled night and climbed into the back of the beautiful antique carriage. A warm wool blanket lay folded on the velvet bench, and they spread it across their laps and snuggled in for the ride. The white lights had been put on the trees throughout downtown immediately following Halloween. Zarina could not believe how early these holidays lights had gone up, but now she appreciated how gorgeous they made their town look at night.

They rode for a while in silence, listening to the clip-clop of the horse hooves on the street. She felt happy. *It's a feeling you almost don't recognize when it comes*, she realized. *If you weren't paying attention, you might not even notice it was there.* A Ferris Bueller quote that communicated this floated in the back of her mind. *If you don't stop and look around once in awhile...* you had to hurry up and enjoy it when it came, because you didn't know when it would come again.

Stan turned to her and began speaking.

"I know that we both think marriage is old-fashioned and stupid," he said, "but one of the things I love about us is that we're old fashioned and stupid. You don't have to say yes, you don't even have to say anything. But I got this for you, and if ever one day you do feel like getting married, I hope it is me you choose to do something old-fashioned and stupid with."

He opened the black velvet box, and she heard the words he was saying but she couldn't believe what was happening. It was like she had fallen asleep and was dreaming. Marriage? Say anything? What?

She looked down at a small but stunning vintage diamond set in white gold filigree. He knew that everything she loved was vintage.

We're both so young, she thought. *How could we possibly know today that we want to spend the rest of our lives together?*

She looked into his sweet, puppy-dog eyes. He actually

crammed himself down onto one knee inside the tiny carriage.

"Zarina," he said. "You're my favorite. Marry me."

She looked at the ring. It sparkled from the white lights from the trees all around.

"You're my favorite, too," she said. "But let's take a little time to think about a wedding, ok?"

He looked at her, devastated as he quietly closed the box. He had no words. And the horses' hooves began to drum their way through the town, deafeningly loud against the silence inside the carriage.

"I CANNOT fucking believe you were in the same theatre with your ex and your beau at the same time during *fucking Cabaret*," said Wes, curling himself into the orange 60s egg pop art chair at Maggie's shop.

"How seriously Broadway was that?" Maggie walked out from behind the counter and sat in the matching egg chair.

"Well you would've made Liza proud if she had been there, for damn sure," said Wes.

"I should've never had that third drink," said Maggie. "Two at dinner and one at the theatre would have been plenty. Buzzed but not trashed, always my goal. The second rum and Coke at intermission was completely unnecessary."

"You mean that confidence juice that made you march up to your ex-husband while he was on a date and cause a scene in the lobby of the theatre? The one that made the intermission more dramatic than the movie?" asked Wes.

"It was not a *scene*, exactly," said Maggie. "I was just introducing everyone."

"Let me paraphrase," said Wes. "I believe your words were something to the effect of 'Oh, hey Dave, this is the guy I'm fucking, Ted.' And then you motioned to Dave's date and said 'Ted, this is the girl who is fucking my husband.' You actually *put your hand out* like she was going to shake yours. *Hilarious.*"

"Total fucking disaster," said Maggie.

"You could hear the awkward silence from a mile around," said Wes. "We couldn't have shown the second half of the movie until the real live drama was done in the lobby, because that's what everyone really wanted to see."

"I don't drink that much," said Maggie, "but when I do, the very thin filter between my brain and my mouth is completely obliterated."

"Truth serum for sure, honey," said Wes. "But maybe it's better that everything is out in the open now?"

"They were on a *first date*," said Maggie. "The poor girl looked horrified. For all she knew he was still married to me, not divorced from me for a decade."

"And what about Ted?" asked Wes. "How did he take it?"

"He laughed when it happened," said Maggie, "I think because he was trying to do the 'oh, silly Maggie had too many drinks' cover-up thing. But I do believe he was shocked at my use of the word 'husband' in reference to my first, *not to mention my second,* my first husband. We fought about it a little bit…"

"Uh oh," said Wes. "Trouble in paradise?"

"He is being ridiculous with this whole 'running away with the band' thing," said Maggie. "I mean, really, he's going to be 50 and he's going to get in a bus and drive across the country to play gigs for chrissakes?"

"Oh, yeah, that's *so* annoying that he wants to risk his boring 9 to 5 job to pursue his dream of music because he has a shot at making it in the nation's number one music industry city. *How rude,*" snarked Wes.

"Why does everyone leave me?" asked Maggie in a quiet voice.

"Oh sweetie, no one leaves you," said Wes. "You leave them. You're always the one in control, right? You left Dave because the two of you didn't know how to be married again after losing a child. You left Matt because he bored you to fucking tears and you'd rather be alone than be in a building with that man for another minute. And if Ted goes to Nashville he won't be *leaving here* as much as *going somewhere* but you'll probably leave him to punish him for leaving you."

"Fuck you," said Maggie, sniffling, "for knowing me so well and for your honesty."

"It's such a lonely word," said Wes.

"Yeah, everyone is so untrue, aren't they, Billy Joel?" said Maggie. Wes could always make her smile. Incorporating Billy Joel lyrics into conversations was something they had been doing for the decade they'd been best friends- in fact it started at a party where they were both quoting a song and no one else recognized it; they'd smiled at each other and that was the beginning of this beautiful friendship.

"You know what I think your problem is?" asked Wes.

"Oh, Christ, please do tell," said Maggie.

"You don't ever want to admit that you need someone," said Wes. "Little Miss Independent. God forbid you're vulnerable and you cry and fall into a man's arms, because your bra-burning mother's generation told you poor little Gloria Steinems to grow dicks so you never had to need one from a man."

"Paging Dr. Freud," said Maggie, laughing, "and fuck you again by the way. What the fuck are you, taking shrink school on the Internet?"

"No," said Wes. "What the fuck I am is right. If you are still in love with the man you have now publicly referred to as your husband even though you haven't worn his ring in a damn decade, then you better take a look in the mirror, sweetie. Stop trying to pretend you're a lesbian, too, because that annoys the shit out of real lesbians. They don't go around sleeping with your potential boyfriends, so you shouldn't be playing 'come on down' like it's the Price is Right with their potential girlfriends."

"I am not trying to pretend I'm a lesbian," said Maggie. "I was just having a bi-curious interaction. I think they call it *experimenting*?"

"Oh, actually when you're sleeping with everyone, I think they call it being a slut," said Wes. "Experimenting is for rats."

"I am not sleeping with everyone," said Maggie.

"But I think there's only one person you want to be sleeping with," said Wes. "And it sure isn't the one with the tits."

EVA DROVE over the drawbridge to Matthew's Island with tears in her eyes. Normally, she felt emotional due to the happiness and relief of crossing the bridge to a more peaceful side of the waters. It felt like the end of the earth, really, leaving behind a faster-paced world on the other side, behind her. But this time she cried as she crossed it because her mother wouldn't be at the cottage to welcome her.

It wasn't her first time back since the accident; of course she'd been back there with Joe and the boys for the funeral and burial, and to take care of things like mail and newspapers. Her mom's cats and the houseplants had been looked after every few days by the cleaning lady, but she needed to spend the weekend at the cottage to decide "what was going to happen next." Would she sell the place? What would she do with all her mom's things?

She pulled into the Matthew's Island Country Store. On the island there were three restaurants, a few carry-out places, and the country store; her favorite place. Patty and Jack, who had bought the store a few years before, had created something completely rare in today's world: a sense of place. They'd respected the history of the store. Its original wooden shelves, sagging slightly under a century of supplies, still held flour and canned goods and trash bags. But they'd incorporated local art and local wines and excellent homemade prepared foods and baked goods so the store had a modern feel as well. It was the perfect blend of old and new, and Eva bought everything from them when she was visiting. Local watermen brought fresh crabmeat and oysters caught in the Chesapeake Bay, and a local creamery delivered ice cream in an amazing array of flavors.

Patty and Jack always greeted her, and all their customers, by name. They knew she'd order the London Broil on a plain wrap with their homemade horseradish sauce. They knew she'd go to the freezer in the back to see what new flavors of homemade ice cream had arrived.

There was comfort in familiarity. Even though she wasn't on the island but maybe once a month, everyone locally seemed to know her and no one treated her like a tourist (what islanders often referred to as a "chicken necker" or an "up-the-roader").

Eva took the short drive to her mother's cottage. *My cottage*, she corrected herself. Once the will had been executed, of course the cottage had been bequeathed to her as the only child. Her mom didn't have any money, just enough to cover the expenses of her death and burial, but she had this cottage. *Her home.* And now it was Eva's.

She drove toward the southern tip of the island and turned left on Tilghman's Neck road. Many years ago, before a population decline, Matthew's Island had consisted of four small villages. Tilghman Neck was one of them. There was still a small church and post office (though now residences) and even though the entire island was only four miles long, the small village with its cluster of 20-25 houses had an even cozier feel to it. She pulled into the driveway.

The cottage sat at the end of the drive, off to itself a bit, nestled near some loblolly pine trees and constructed diagonally to face the water. Built in 1932, it was a Cape Cod-style house with arts and crafts styling, though no truly high form of architecture existed on the provincial island. There was a screened front porch with a vintage 1930s metal porch furniture set: a three seat glider, two rocking chairs and a matching table. She entered the porch, always appreciating the *thwap* of the wooden screen door behind her. The extra key was "hidden" under a jar of seafoam green sea glass on the coffee table. She used this key, forgetting that she had her mom's set in her purse now.

Eva's mom had been a great decorator, achieving the perfect "coastal style" after devouring books and magazines on the décor for years. The soft aqua, yellow, orange and cream hues throughout the cottage creating a soothing environment and a perfect backdrop for her sea glass and driftwood accents. Eva put the groceries away in the small retro red and white kitchen with its small chrome metal table and vinyl and chrome chairs. She stopped and stared at the table. It was like the ghost of her mom was sitting there, drinking her coffee and reading the newspaper like she did every day for fifty years, the last several decades alone since her husband had died.

Every moment she remembered her mom wasn't coming back felt like a punch to the stomach. Being in the cottage alone was strange. It wasn't bad, it was just different. Quiet, peaceful, a tiny bit spooky. She would have to learn how to be alone. She was used to noisy worlds: teenage boys, industrious big city law firms. When she'd left this island at age 18, she swore she would never come back. After growing up in such a small place, she wanted nothing but big cities. But now, the smallness of it all created a completely perfect place for her to try to put the pieces of her life back together, somehow.

She sat down at the small table to eat her meal. Taking out her iPad, she put on her Pandora Motown station for background noise, and did the first thing she always did when she got to the cottage: she checked the tide schedule. As any good sea glass hunter knew, low tide was the best time of the day to find the shards of bottles and tableware from years past. Enormous antique apothecary jars like the one in her office, filled with sea glass in colors that matched each room's décor around the cottage, awaited her new beach finds after they were cleaned and dried and sorted. Tomorrow morning, she knew where she'd be at 9:10 a.m.: on the beach, picking up the broken pieces.

LISA WALKED into the downtown restaurant and saw Ben sitting at the bar. She immediately recognized the blazer, jeans, brown hair and that fabulous smile with that goddamn distracting dimple as he got up from his seat and turned to face her. *That dimple*, she had written in her diary, *is so entrancing.* She walked over and he reached out to embrace her. He held on to her for a second longer than casual business acquaintances or friends would do, and she breathed in his smell. It was familiar, and she felt a shiver through her spine as he stepped away.

"So what do beautiful bakers like to drink?" asked Ben, looking into her face intently with those gypsy hazel eyes. "Vanilla vodka? Chocolate liqueur?"

"Beer," said Lisa, smiling at him. "It's pumpkin ale season, and there's a local brew I love."

"Sounds great. I'll try one, too," said Ben. "Do you want to get an appetizer here at the bar, or should we get a table?"

"Oh, let's stay here and get an appetizer," Lisa said. She was too nervous to sit at a table—any one of her customers or her stupid subdivision neighbors could walk in, and sitting at the bar with someone who wasn't your husband seemed so much less formal than having a table to themselves.

They ordered the crab dip with homemade Old Bay chips, a Maryland staple, and some calamari. The pumpkin ales arrived and they sipped from the bottles.

"So you haven't told me much about your husband," said Ben.

"Well, he's a real estate developer in DC, so he's gone a lot," said Lisa, and then she found herself blurting out, "and he has a foot fetish, which is really awful since I have a whole closet full of shoes I don't even wear. I'd rather turn them all into cast iron cookware or a new Viking stove or a college fund."

Ben laughed softly. "I'm sorry," he said, "I don't mean to laugh. But I think that's more words in a row than I've ever heard you say."

Lisa blushed and said, "I'm sorry."

"Don't be," said Ben. "I like the idea of getting to know you. And that sucks about the whole shoe thing. I've heard of foot fetishes but I don't know much about them and I wasn't even sure they were a real thing. I guess they are."

"Oh, it's real," said Lisa. "Believe me. I probably have $40,000 worth of shoes that say it's real. Too bad he doesn't have a flip-flop fetish. I prefer wearing those."

"Well, you might have your Viking stove that way, I guess," said Ben.

"So what about you, mystery man?" said Lisa. "We're

friends on Facebook but I feel like I don't know you. I find out you have a son, and honestly, I don't even know if you're single or secretly married or what." For some reason, talking about Jim and her feet had made her more conversationally bold.

"I was with Max's mom for a long time," said Ben. "But she left over a year ago."

"Oh, Ben," said Lisa. "I'm sorry."

"I don't really have personal pictures on my Facebook account because I have clients for friends, and I don't like having pictures of Max on the Internet for some reason. I used to have family pictures up, but after she left, I couldn't stand to have them there anymore."

"That sounds tough," said Lisa. "And now you're a single dad?"

"It's not easy," said Ben. "But Max is absolutely the coolest little guy in the world, so it really isn't as difficult as it could be."

Their food arrived. They ate together, sharing stories about their siblings, their jobs, their neighborhoods. But it was getting late. Ben had to pick Max up at the preschool's aftercare program, and Lisa wanted to be home before Jim got home.

He walked her to her car near the bakery.

"Thanks for a nice evening, Lisa," said Ben, looking down at her, the shadow of that dimple more pronounced in the streetlight.

She looked up at him.

"No, thank you," she said. "I enjoy spending time with you."

And then he took her hand in his and leaned down and kissed her. Ever so gently, right on the mouth, right on the street where anyone could drive by and see. It wasn't a long kiss, it almost could have been mistaken from a distance as a friendly goodbye kiss, but it was just long enough for her to feel it all the way inside her body and wish it went on forever and ever or at least for a few hours, preferably while naked.

"Goodnight, Lisa," said Ben as he gently released her hand.

"Goodnight, Ben," said Lisa.

LISA WAS a few minutes early for the November meeting of the Scarlet Letter Society. She parked her Chevy Equinox (Cyber Metallic Gray; she'd bought the 2010 car used, swearing she wasn't thinking about it being roomy enough for a baby) a few blocks over at the bakery where she'd walk back to work after the meeting.

Zarina saw Lisa as she walked up the street toward the shop, holding the door open to let her in.

"I know I'm a little early, Zarina," said Lisa. "Sorry."

"Why would you be sorry, silly?" said Zarina. "Come on in and get warm by the fake fire and tell me what kind of coffee you want. You think everyone is sick of the pumpkin lattes we drank all through October? I did break out the peppermint mocha latte. Too soon?"

"No way," said Lisa. "It's never too soon for a peppermint mocha latte. I could drink them all year. I never understand why they have to be a holiday thing."

"So what's new with you?" Zarina asked, sitting down next to her.

"Oh, I don't know," said Lisa. "I'm stuck in this place of trying to decide whether I should fight for my marriage. We're thinking about going to marriage counseling. And then whether we would go for in vitro so I can have the baby I've been wanting for what seems like forever. Or, I could just go ahead and have a passionate love affair with my graphic designer, get pregnant with his love child, and Jim would never know the difference."

"Whoa, there," said Zarina. "Back that train up for a second. What do you mean go ahead and have one? Haven't you been having one for months? I seem to recall something about walk-in freezer and covered bridge sex."

Lisa turned crimson red, as though her internal temperature instantly rose 10 degrees.

"Oh my God," she said. "I am such an idiot. You can't say anything to Maggie or Eva. They would throw me out of SLS."

"Chill," Zarina said. "I'm not going to tell anybody anything. Do you mind me asking why in the hell you want to be a member of the Scarlet Letter Society in the first place when you aren't even cheating on your husband?"

"I've thought about cheating on him for a year," said Lisa. "I have a guy I would cheat with, and actually he kissed me last night for the first time. I have no friends in my subdivision. When I met Maggie and Lisa in the shop last year, I really liked them and I wanted to fit in. I overheard them talking about boyfriends versus husbands, and I just sort of…"

"You just sort of completely lied to get into the group," Zarina said. "You know, if they knew about this, they would probably just laugh it off, but don't worry. Your secret is safe with me. I have enough problems of my own without blabbering about yours."

"So what else is up?" asked Lisa, happy to change the subject.

"Stan asked me to marry him," said Zarina, frowning at the memory of how the night went.

"Isn't that supposed to be a wonderful thing?" asked Lisa.

"I guess it's supposed to be," said Zarina. "Or it would've been, if I'd said yes."

"Oh, gosh, you said no," said Lisa. "Yikes. Wow. Why?"

"I don't even think I know," said Zarina. "I just don't think I'm ready for marriage. I love Stan, but I hate the thought of the dress, and the paperwork…"

"I understand," said Lisa. "So did you guys break up?"

"Stan summoned enough of his poor humiliated ego to

say he was fine with giving me some time to think about it," said Zarina, "but it's been super awkward."

"It's ok to need time to think about something as major as marriage," said Lisa. "Don't feel guilty about it. You have to think of yourself first and what you want. This is a lifelong decision. Trust me."

"Thanks, Lisa," said Zarina.

Maggie and Eva walked in.

"Well you girls look cozy," said Eva. "What are you over here chatting about?"

"Just deciding how many of Zarina's gingerbread muffins I'm going to buy to bring over to the bakery," said Lisa. "Her stuff flies off the shelf faster than my own."

"Yep, just getting Lisa's muffin situation worked out," Zarina said, and winked at her as she walked over to the counter to prepare coffee for the ladies.

"Well I would like to have that peppermint mocha," said Lisa, glancing at the chalkboard sign on the counter. "Never too early."

"Yum," said Maggie.

"Make it three," said Eva.

"I made both gingerbread and pumpkin cheesecake muffins in mini size," I said. "So you could sample."

"Thanks, Z," said Maggie, settling in with the other women in their cozy chatting spot. "So what do you girls think of this book, *The Awakening* by Kate Chopin?" asks Maggie.

"Well, I read it," said Eva, and acknowledging the surprised glances around her, added, "I know, it's becoming a habit. And really? *More goddamn death*? Suicides? You gotta be kidding me."

"Agreed," said Lisa, as she took out her beloved journal. Before she flipped back to her notes on the book, she smiled when she read her most recent entry, only a few words scrawled the night before: *'Is there any going back?'*

"But there is so much beautiful language in the book," said Lisa. "Listen to this gorgeous prose:

'The voice of the sea is seductive; never ceasing, whispering, clearing, murmuring, inviting the soul to wander for a spell in the abysses of solitude; to lose itself in mazes of inward contemplation. The voice of the sea speaks to the soul. The touch of the sea is sensuous, enfolding the body in its soft, close embrace.'

"Yeah, the sea is fantastic," said Eva. "Right up until you drown yourself in it."

"But this one doesn't seem to off herself as much out of guilt," said Maggie. "She's stronger."

"*'Perhaps it is better to wake up after all, even to suffer, rather than to remain a dupe to illusions all one's life,'*" read Lisa. I also like the line, *'but whatever came, she had resolved never again to belong to another than herself.'*"

"She does seem more likeable as a feminist character," said Eva. "Too bad she has to die over it."

Zarina delivered the platter of small muffins, then the coffee.

Suddenly Wes came dashing into the coffee shop. He greeted the other women but headed directly to Maggie.

"Sorry for interrupting your little Ho-prah book club," he said. "But I have news. Alfred and I have decided to celebrate the passage of gay marriage in Maryland by getting gay married!"

There were screams of joy and applause.

"Holy Big Gay Wedding!" declared Maggie. "Are you serious? That's amazing! Congratulations!" She jumped up from her spot on the couch to hug him.

"December 31 at midnight, the moment the marriage equality law goes into effect in Maryland," said Wes, beaming from ear to ear as he looked around the coffee shop. "And you're all invited!"

December 2012

"There's a girl right next to you/And she's just waiting
for something to do. When you can't be with the one you
love/Honey, Love the one you're with."
-"Love the One You're With," Stephen Stills

Monthly meeting of the Scarlet Letter Society.
Canceled
See you on New Year's Eve!

With Christmas and a wedding this month, we'll skip the meeting
and take Wes out for a groom's lunch instead. It's like a bridal
shower, but with a hot gay groom.

"The scarlet letter was her passport into regions where
other women dared not tread."
-*The Scarlet Letter*, Nathaniel Hawthorne

from: **Kate** kfredericks@CarrollCollege.edu

to: **Maggie** mags@wingsvintage.com

date: Tuesday, November 20, 2012, 11:07 PM

subject: Hey gorgeous

How was your day? Can't stop thinking about you. Another lunch soon?

Xo

Kate

Maggie lay on her sofa in her flannel pjs, Tosh.0 on the tv in the background, her cats Steinbeck (the mouser) and Grizabella curled up with her and her soft blanket. Her Orange Pekoe tea rested on the table beside her. She had cleaned the apartment for the Thanksgiving arrival of her two girls the next day. Dave was already in New York picking up Lilith from Syracuse; they'd drive back to Maryland in the morning. Maggie knew Lily was ready for the break from her freshman year. Erica, a senior at Western Maryland University, would be driving home in the morning.

The girls would be staying in Maggie's spare bedroom tomorrow night. There were two twin beds for the rare occasion they were home at the same time. Normally, they stayed with Dave. The stone Queen Anne Victorian on Clark Avenue in Keytown had remained unsold after the divorce. Dave still lived there, and the girls' original bedrooms remained intact. They'd gotten rid of most of the nasty old stuffed animals, but a few remnants of their childhood remained. The girls would stay there after Thanksgiving dinner. Dave had invited Maggie to eat dinner with them, and she had accepted. Normally they split their time with the girls, but it would nice to have a meal together as a 'family' even though technically their family had been broken years before. It would be peaceful now.

from:	**Maggie** mags@wingsvintage.com
to:	**Kate** kfredericks@CarrollCollege.edu
date:	Tuesday, November 20, 2012, 11:14 PM
subject:	Hey there

Super busy with girls coming home from respective higher education establishments. Catch up next week sometime. Happy Thanksgiving!

Maggie

Maggie knew the tone in her email didn't match Kate's flirtier one. She felt bad, but she was unsure of what tone to use in the relationship. Kate was obviously interested in continuing their affair, and Maggie was confused about what she wanted. It had been fun to try, she liked Kate as a person, and she didn't want to rule out anything in the future. Really though, she didn't think she wanted to have an ongoing love affair with a woman and wasn't sure what to do with the relationship while she figured out what was going on with the rest of her complicated love life. She didn't think it was going to be a long-term thing, and there wasn't any easy way to be friends with Kate without the sex. They'd only been together a few times, and Maggie had been turned on by it, but the intensity of the new relationship had scared Maggie a bit, especially while she was in a state of confusion over how to handle Ted.

She didn't want to completely shut Kate out of her life, but her instinct now was to buy time until she could figure it all out. For now, she just wanted to watch Daniel Tosh with her purring cats and wait for her beautiful, somehow-all-grown-up girls to get there.

She sipped her tea and closed her laptop.

"I LOVE the idea of a New Year's Eve wedding," said Wes, "a new beginning." Knowing they both loved her vintage stuff, Maggie had invited Wes and Alfred to come over to the shop and pick out a few fantastic vintage tuxes for free as her gift to them.

"Especially on the first night of the state's legalization of gay marriage," Wes continued, "even though it will be a mad rush to throw the whole event together. What a fantastic time to celebrate; the turn of a new year, to turn a new page."

"Well I'm glad we will at least be living in one of only 9 states in the country to legalize what should be common SENSE law in all 50," said Alfred as he flipped through a floral design book they'd brought to Maggie's shop.

Alfred hadn't loved the idea of people making a big deal out it, or even the idea of a big wedding. His parents were gone, and his brother was a homophobic conservative Republican who didn't acknowledge Wes' existence. The whole wedding would be about 25 people, which the men agreed was the perfect size for two aging gay theatre geeks.

"I can't believe you have actual choices in vintage tuxes that are close enough to our sizes. And we even have enough time to get a few quick alterations and have them ready in time for this wedding," yelled Wes from the dressing room.

"Yeah, well you're lucky I have a seamstress on speed dial willing to work a rush job at Christmas," yelled Maggie back.

Wes came out of the dressing room in a midnight blue velvet tux complete with ruffles and bow tie, and the way he worked the room like it was a fashion runway made her laugh hysterically.

Alfred rolled his eyes.

"You're seriously going to wear that to our wedding?" he said.

"Only if it pisses you off," said Wes, laughing at his Brad Pitt look-alike husband to be. "Of course you will need a matching apricot colored one so we look just like Jim Carrey and Jeff Daniels in 'Dumb and Dumber.'"

"That sounds perfect for a Big Gay Wedding," said Alfred. He was about to go into the dressing room with a more traditional black Frank-Sinatra style tux. When he came out of the dressing room wearing a more casual shirt, unbuttoned and no tie, Maggie and Wes gasped.

"Yeah, I know," joked Alfred. "I'm smoking hot."

They all laughed.

One of Maggie's customers was what Maggie called "some kind of hippie reverend who probably does more Reiki and yoga than reverend-ing," but she was legal. She'd introduced the woman to Wes and Alfred, who were planning to write their own vows for the brief ceremony.

A bunch of actors and set designers from the theatre had volunteered to decorate the location: Catoctin Cottage was a lodge style log cabin with a single enormous room: huge stone fireplace, vaulted beam ceilings, and an amazing view of the mountains. The state park system normally had it closed for the winter, but as a favor to Maggie, Dave had made a call from his historic preservation office over to the park service and they'd agreed to let them use it.

Lisa was going to work with a caterer friend (and of course she was making the cakes; there would be small wedding cakes at the center of each table) to put together a small reception after the ceremony. The room was actually big enough to have the ceremony in front of the fireplace and the reception in the other half of the room. Simple, easy, small. That's what the grooms wanted.

Wes was beaming. He told Maggie he was happiest about Alfred moving in. Rings and license papers aside, he loved that they wouldn't have to exist in their separate spaces anymore. Their toothbrushes would be together. They hated the nights when one of them would leave, and they couldn't wait until they wouldn't have to leave ever again.

RON OPENED the door to his Dupont Circle apartment and stepped aside to allow Eva to enter. He closed the door behind them. She held a bag containing their breakfast: bagels and cream cheese and lox, two large coffees.

"Thanks for bringing breakfast," he said. He was dressed for work, though his shirt was unbuttoned. When he'd gone to button it a few moments earlier he realized that was probably a silly thing to do under the circumstances.

She put the breakfast on the table and walked over to him. Stepping up on her tippy toes, she kissed him on the cheek and tousled his hair. It was an odd gesture, one that reminded her of the exact thing she did to her teenage sons after a lacrosse game or before they left for the day. Calvin never minded; Graham always shook her off—he didn't want the Axe products in his hair disturbed. When she'd started seeing Ron, she had quickly calculated the age difference between him and her sons. It was a comfortable 16 years, but she was still practically old enough to be Ron's mother.

He kissed her. It was a gentle, lingering kiss and she returned it with the same slow pace. They hadn't been seeing much of each other. Since her mother's death, she'd taken leave and had spent most of her time either at the cottage sorting through belongings or home with the boys. She hadn't been in the DC office in weeks and was headed there today.

"I'm more than happy to bring breakfast," Eva told Ron. "It's been awhile."

"I missed you," said Ron.

"I missed you, too," said Eva. "But my life got a little crazy there for awhile."

"I am so, so sorry that you lost your mom," said Ron. He walked to the table and spread out the breakfast for them, grabbing mugs to pour the coffee into so they wouldn't have to drink out of paper cups.

"Thanks," said Eva. "It's been a tough time, but it gave me a lot of time to myself to think about my life and where it's headed."

"Did you come to any conclusions?" said Ron.

"I work too much," replied Eva. "I want to spend more time with my boys because before I know it, they'll be gone. Even though part of me is sad about it, I want my marriage to officially end. No marriage at all is better than the façade of a marriage. Joe has agreed to a divorce."

"I guess you knew that was coming eventually," said Ron.

"Yeah, something about my mom's death made me realize I can't go through life in some kind of coma as though I have no control over my own outcome," said Eva. "I need to be happy."

"You do," said Ron. He walked over and hugged her. "You deserve to be happy."

"And I should thank you," said Eva. "Because you have made me happy in the months we've known each other."

He kissed her in response. Talking about their relationship was not something he was comfortable with or good at. She attributed it to his age. Normally, this was fine. They were too busy having sex to sit around and discuss their feelings. But now, she was in a place in her life where she needed to know where things stood, or to decide to put them there herself.

But his hands were on her blouse now, and she felt herself get aroused. She decided to allow herself the luxury and the escape of being with Ron again, even though for some time she'd known it wouldn't last. She knew this was goodbye sex, and she decided to enjoy it. He suddenly lifted her up and took her to the bedroom.

"Guess we'll need to warm up that coffee in a little bit," said Eva.

"That's what microwaves are for," said Ron.

He placed her gently on the bed. She ran her hands across his chest, down that great "V" towards his stiffness, and she undid his belt. While he took off his pants and shirt, laying them neatly on a chair, she got up and took off her own work clothes.

They made love to each other, not with the great passion and urgency they normally had, but with tenderness and caring. Theirs had been an amazing love affair, one they would each always remember fondly and even though neither of them talked about it ending, each of them knew it would. There was no reason for a bitter breakup, nasty words or drama. They'd each appreciate and remember the time they'd shared together, and hold the memory of each other in their own hearts forever.

After breakfast, when Eva walked down the building's steps to her office a few blocks away, she remembered seeing the pair of earrings on the coffee table, the pink toothbrush in the bathroom. She knew it was time for Ron to move on, too.

As MAGGIE was browsing through the racks of her own vintage dresses searching for something to wear to the upcoming wedding, the mailman entered the shop. She greeted him as she always did, and they chatted for a few minutes. When he left, she went to place the mail on the counter and noticed one of the letters was from Dewey, Cheetam and Howe. That wasn't the actual name of the law firm, but it was how she always referred to them. Divorces were ridiculously expensive. You could spend more on a divorce than an actual marriage.

Maggie knew what was in the envelope. It was the finalized copies of the executed, notarized divorce from Matt. They'd been married less than two years. Maggie cursed herself for entering into a marriage out of fear of growing old alone. She'd simply been tired of being single. It had been nearly a decade, and she had just wanted someone to take out the trash once in awhile so she didn't have to do it every single time. She didn't think it had mattered that she wasn't in love with Matt. One night when he had suggested a trip to Vegas and an impromptu wedding, she'd agreed despite the feeling in the pit of her stomach. They were companionable enough and maybe it was time, she'd thought, to be with someone with whom there was no emotional drama.

The price for passion was boredom, thought Maggie, *and I was bored beyond words*. She'd moved out of her two floor apartment and into the country. She was a city mouse trying to pretend to be a country mouse, and it didn't go well. It was too quiet on the farm. She hadn't known how accustomed she was to the sounds of her town she was until she didn't hear them anymore. She hadn't moved anything out of her apartment, almost as though she knew she'd be back soon, and one day she just told Matt she wanted to stay in the apartment because she had to be at work early the next day. And it had been as simple as that. She called him that morning, they went to lunch, and she told him she just wasn't happy. She apologized. He was understanding, said he'd been happy to have her as long as he had in his life. This of course only served to make her feel more guilty.

Dave had been shocked to hear of Maggie's wedding, but pretended he wasn't that surprised. *Silly Maggie,* he'd said, as though she ran off and got married on a regular basis. She knew he'd been hurt, and she hadn't meant to hurt him. They'd made love a few times while she was married, and she thought it was funny she was cheating on her second husband with her first. She cheated on everyone with Dave.

"Hey there, first husband," Maggie said, after dialing Dave. "Come over and have lunch with me to celebrate my divorce."

"The one from me or the other guy?" asked Dave. They hadn't spoken for a while after the events in the vacant building and at the theatre, and they both seemed to glad to be "back to normal," even though their normal wasn't what most people considered it to be.

"The other guy, dumbass," said Maggie. "I don't think you're supposed to celebrate a divorce from someone with the actual person you divorced."

"Meet you at the shop in five minutes?"

"Yep," said Maggie. "I was just trying on dresses for the wedding." She pulled out three great dresses from the 50s-60s era to try on in her own dressing room.

Dave had been visiting a building nearby, and hung up the phone as he walked into the shop. He entered the dressing room without asking. She'd heard the shop door open but assumed it was a customer and called, "Be with you in a minute!"

He lifted the heavy brocade curtain fabric aside and quickly walked into the dressing room without sliding the curtain open.

"How about you be with me right *this* minute?" he said.

She laughed. She was in a black bra and a black vintage slip, in between trying on dresses for the wedding. She play-slapped him. "Perv." He turned her around to face the full-length mirror.

"Look how beautiful you are," he said. "You've been the most beautiful woman I've ever seen since the day I met you, a million years ago."

She smiled, looking in the mirror at their reflection. Many more wrinkles on those faces than there were all those years ago, but they still looked about the same, middle age hadn't beaten them up too badly. She reached her arms up over her head to put them around his neck. His shaggy brown hair, glasses and beard combined with his muscular tall frame made him seem like a nerdy but sexy construction worker. He wore construction work boots each day because he entered so many dilapidated buildings, muddy stone cellars, and old barns, often documenting them right before their demolitions.

"Yes," she said. "A million years ago when the dinosaurs roamed."

She turned to face him and started unbuttoning his plaid flannel shirt. The pink velour 60s sofa in the dressing room would be a great place for a quickie if no one entered the shop.

"Customers?" he asked.

"Right now I only have one," said Maggie, running her hands across his hairy chest and smooth ribcage. "Fuck me."

"Yes, ma'am," said Dave, grinning. He unbuckled his jeans. She unclasped her bra, tossing it on the vintage hooked area rug on the floor. She sat on the plush sofa and pulled down his boxer briefs, then used her mouth to arouse him until he was rock hard and moaning with pleasure.

"You are really good to your customers," said Dave.

"Well you're a pretty loyal one," said Maggie, licking him as she said "loyal." She turned around, placing her hands on the pink sofa and lifting the vintage black silk slip as he lowered his jeans. She looked at him in the mirror and said, "Now fuck me."

He placed his big hands on her curvy hips and took her from behind, reaching around to her stimulate her with his strong fingers.

The exploded together quickly and quietly, both worried someone would enter the shop, though no one did. The frenzied dressing room sex left them both flushed.

"Lunchtime!" said Maggie.

"I know, I know, you're always starving after sex," said Dave as they got dressed.

She locked the door of the shop behind them, hanging the "Back at 1:00" sign in the window.

They sat down at an Italian restaurant; the one you had to go down the steps to get to from the street. He knew she'd order the stuffed shells, she knew he'd order the white spinach pizza.

"So how's work?" she asked.

"Oh, you know, just trying to keep an old building or two up," he said.

They talked about the wedding; Maggie jokingly asking if he'd be her date, Dave pretending to have to consider it then acting like he reluctantly agreed.

"Hey, listen. I wanted to ask you about something," said Dave.

"Sure," said Maggie. "What's up, hon?"

"It's Christmas this week and I know you haven't stayed overnight in the house in a long, long time. I don't know how many years. But the girls will both be home and of course you can stay in the guest room if you want, but I just thought, maybe…"

Her eyes filled with tears. She had hated returning to that house because it as where her son had died, along with her marriage to the man she loved.

"Maggie," he said, "I don't want you to cry. If you don't want to, it's ok. I just know that the girls probably won't be coming home for many more holidays, so I thought we could spend Christmas Eve together as a family. For old times' sake."

"I would love to do that," said Maggie. "For old times' sake."

MAGGIE, EVA, Lisa and Wes sat around a table at Vive, the fancy chef-owned place on Commerce Street Wes and Alfred loved to go for dinner. Maggie thought it seemed like an appropriate setting for the small "shower." Eva, Maggie and Lisa had brought gifts, and Wes was chattering on about the details of the wedding.

"I'm glad we did it sooner rather than later," he said, "because I would have driven myself crazy with the hundreds of details you can put into a wedding. I just want to get married to Alfred. I don't want to spend hours obsessing over flowers and photographers."

He cleared his throat and then he turned serious.

"I would like to ask my sort of straight girl best friend something," said Wes. "Margaret Elizabeth, will you be my maid of honor?"

Maggie beamed.

"Of course I will, you big drama queen," she responded. "But only if I get to wear the ugliest bridesmaid dress in my shop."

"You know that's a deal, hunty!" said Wes, grinning at her.

"It seems like everything is falling into place rather nicely," said Eva. "I can't wait to see how beautiful the lodge looks at night on New Year's Eve. What a fantastic night for a wedding."

"Yes, it's the best night of the year for fresh starts," said Maggie.

"It's so romantic," said Lisa. "I just can't wait."

They ordered squash soups, goat cheese terrines, venison stew and other delightful items from the menu, sharing and trying everything like it was a big family meal.

"We had fun picking out a gift for you," said Maggie, after they'd finished sampling homemade eggnog sorbet and peppermint mocha cheesecake. "Though it isn't easy to shop for the men who already have everything."

"We hope you like it," said Lisa.

Eva reached down and handed Wes the box. Inside was a gift certificate for three-day stay at a gorgeous mountaintop lodge and spa not far from the wedding location.

"Oh my God," said Wes. "This can be a mini honeymoon! We weren't going to go away til spring to celebrate, but we can both take a few days off and hang out after the ceremony."

He looked around the table.

"You girls know how to pick out the best gifts," he said, "but seriously, I love you all. Thank you so much. Now who's ready for a wedding?" The three women smiled, raising their glasses in unison. Despite their own challenges in their own marriages, he could see in their eyes that each of them still believed in love and couldn't have been happier for him.

On December 31, everything seemed to be lining up perfectly. Once the clock struck midnight, Wes and Alfred would be allowed to legally marry. The reverend had the paperwork with her from the court. Catoctin Cottage lodge was stunning, with hundreds of white candles in every shape and size forming a ring around the room. Striped monotone white and cream linens on the four round tables matched the creams and whites of the flowers in the crystal bowls of water beside the perfect mini-wedding cakes on each table. The centerpieces actually sparkled, clearly aided by crystals or some magical bling that had been added by the theatre designers. White votive candles lined every windowsill, and even more candles stood on the tables.

The enormous stone mantel of the massive two-story stone fireplace was lined with white pillar candles of every height, and draped in the front with a floral swag of ivory roses, magnolia leaves and ivy. An enormous iron chandelier hung from the ceiling, lit by a dozen cream pillar candles. There was no electrical lighting in the room. There was no need. The glow was amazing and the photographer, a friend of Alfred's, was ready to capture the beautiful lighting.

Wes walked in and saw Alfred standing by the fireplace in his gorgeous vintage Armani black tux, tousled hair and open shirt. He looked every bit the part of the Hollywood hunk. Any doubt either might have had about the ceremony melted away like candle wax. Anyone in the room could see that the love in their eyes matched the love they felt in their hearts. Wes walked over and kissed his groom. The crowd roared, clinking glasses.

"Let's do this," Wes said.

Theatre friends had agreed to provide simple acoustic music during the ceremony. They actually played the bridal march as the two men walked in together, and the room was filled with laughter at their dance moves, taking turns "twirling" each other across the room.

The small group of friends and family gathered around the fire. Large electric heaters had been added on the other side of the room. Though the lodge wasn't heated, the warmth of the fire was perfect to keep everyone warm on the cold, dark winter night at the beautiful lodge on the mountain.

It took less than fifteen minutes for Wes and Alfred to exchange rings, pledge their love and make eternal vows. They'd written the touching words themselves, but had agreed to keep it brief: only three sentences apiece. (*"Like a Twitter wedding,"* Wes had joked).

"I promise to never let us run out of microwave popcorn when we watch scary movies," said Wes. "I will never forget, no matter how many years go by, to tell you that you are amazing and gorgeous and how much I love you. And I vow to cherish you and hold you in my heart forever because you are my world."

And Alfred told Wes, "I promise to make you coffee every morning, even though I still can't believe you use all that icky cream and sugar. I will love you the very best way I possibly can until the very last day I have. And I will never stop appreciating how at peace I am when I am in your arms."

Their embrace went on for a few more moments, and amongst cheers of "Kiss the Groom," they kissed.

The reverend's words were also touching:

"May your hearts be as one. Blessings abound when you cherish unconditional love. When troubles come, God's power will be your strength and courage. Know the joy of each other's love. May your hearts be as one: Divine."

These were words they would always remember on a night they could never forget.

And when the ceremony was over, the two men snuck away from the small group for a private moment outside on the large stone deck overlooking the lights of the city below from the mountain where they were perched on this New Year's Eve.

"I love you," said Wes. "And now it's official and legal and the other 41 states can go straight to hell."

"They sure can," Alfred said, smiling. "And I know for sure that I love you right back."

And as they embraced, kissing as husband and husband, they looked out over the dark forest and saw that it had begun to snow.

January 2013

"I have a face I cannot show
I make the rules up as I go
Just try and love me if you can.
Are you strong enough to be my man?"
- "Strong Enough," Sheryl Crow

Monthly meeting of the Scarlet Letter Society.
*Blackbirds Pie shop
Friday, January 4, 2013
5:30 a.m.

*Since Zarina and Stanley have disappeared for a sudden vacation week together, apparently inspired by the divine wedding of Wes and Alfred, we will meet at Lisa's shop. Fuck all the slut-shaming guilt and death in the books we've been reading. No book this *month; it's on hiatus until we find something more upbeat to read. Happy New Year, all!*

"The scarlet letter was her passport into regions where other women dared not tread."
-The Scarlet Letter, **Nathaniel Hawthorne**

Eva saw the email from Maggie and smiled despite her somber locale. She sat in the chair opposite Joe as they waited to sign their divorce paperwork. She had been pleasantly surprised at the speed with which the paperwork had been drawn up. Joe had admitted adultery so that they could obtain an instant divorce. She thought that was ironic considering the degree to with she'd been unfaithful as well.

"Are you smiling because our marriage is over?" Joe asked, not in an unkind way.

"No, Joe," Eva responded. "I was smiling at an email from Maggie. I am absolutely not happy our marriage is over. 15 years is a long time to be with someone and have it come to an end. I think it's sad."

"I am not sure where exactly we went wrong," said Joe. "But I want you to know that I wish I could have been a better husband, and I hope this all goes peacefully and we can remain friends."

"Thanks, Joe," said Eva. "I haven't by any stretch been the best wife, either. We're always going to be the parents of our boys, and that will never change, so I think it would be a lot easier and certainly a lot nicer if we remained friends. I don't see any reason why we shouldn't."

"Me either," said Joe.

They'd already discussed the arrangement with the house and boys. They would share custody. Joe would stay at an apartment in Baltimore near the hospital, and Eva was moving to the cottage, where the boys would visit her most weekends. She planned to fix up the guest house for them. Joe and Eva would each have a bedroom at the house in Keytown, and they'd alternate caretaking of the boys from there for the next few years until they were off to college. This way the boys didn't have to move from their home during high school.

The boys had taken it well, surprising both Joe and Eva with their maturity. Calvin had said the most important thing was that they were each happy, which had brought tears to Eva's eyes, and Graham had nodded his head in agreement. There was no doubt it was a sad ending, but the four of them agreed that they'd always be family, and that this was what was important. Despite their efforts to put a big-boy face on it, Eva could see the hurt and anger the boys felt. She worried about how it would affect them, whether they would act out.

And so, in less than 30 minutes in a well-appointed but chilly law office and the signing of a twelve-page document in triplicate, a marriage was over.

MAGGIE AND Ted took their coffees from the barista and found a table in "The Other Coffee Shop," which is what she called the Starbucks downtown. She rarely set foot in the place, obviously preferring Z's. For many years, the debate about whether the big chain should even be allowed to open their rubber-stamp coffee shop in the historic town raged. Some people thought it would destroy the small-town charm, others thought it was a sign the state's second biggest city had arrived and besides, Starbucks was renovating a gorgeous old place, not tearing something down to build something new. Ultimately, the chain won. It had clearly permeated the nation's coffee psyche, and not enough people were that passionately against the idea. Besides, Z's business never suffered. A town couldn't have too may coffee shops and her shop's funky vibe was preferred by most locals to the mermaid with the wavy hair.

"So I have news," said Ted.

"Oh yeah?" asked Maggie.

"I quit my job," he said. "And I'm leaving on a jet plane."

"Nashville," Maggie said, and she smiled, because she knew it meant he was following his dream.

"Yep," he said. "I can't believe a bunch of middle aged guys like us are pulling up roots and running away with our garage band like teenagers, but we are."

"I had a feeling you'd go for it," said Maggie. "And good for you. I will miss you, but it's sure been fun to have you around."

"Ah, Mags," said Ted. "I'm gonna write a song about you. You're the kinda girl a guy only meets once, and should write a song about."

"Awshucks, Ted," Maggie said playfully. "That's a very sweet thing to say."

And then she heard a familiar voice.

"Well look who it is," said Wes, walking over with his mocha latte. "This one never shows her face in here." He looked at Ted and tilted his head toward Maggie.

"You know Zarina is closed today," said Maggie. "Sit down."

"Sure I'm not interrupting anything?" said Wes.

"Nah, have a seat," said Ted.

"Now all we need is whatshername and we'll have a real party," said Wes, looking at Maggie.

"Kate?" said Maggie. "Her name is Kate. And fortunately for you, Ted knows about her now."

"Yeah, Mags, what is going on with the professor?" said Ted. "You girls still gettin it on?"

"Do tell," said Wes.

"Hoo-ha is complicated," said Maggie. "It was a fun place to visit, and I wouldn't rule out future encounters with women, but I'm not sure I want to live there."

"That's what I always said, and I didn't even like the visit," said Wes, making a gagging motion.

Ted looked at Maggie.

"Well, I guess we're all 'friends of Maggie' here," he said, "so I have another question. What's going on with you and that first husband of yours?"

"I guess the same thing that's always been going on," said Maggie. "What do you mean?"

"I think you still love him," said Ted.

"Well, duh, she's cheated on every damn guy she's been with for Dave and only Dave," said Wes. "Why not *just* do Dave?"

Maggie felt awkward talking about this in front of Ted — they'd never really discussed her feelings for Dave. But now her life would be less complicated since he was leaving, without the need for some childish breakup. They could store away their time together, be thankful for it, and move on.

"I *am* doing Dave," she said. "I even spent the night in the old house."

"Oh, Lordy," said Wes. "That's a big one."

"Yeah," said Maggie, "I know."

"You know what I think?" said Ted. "I think you're so used to being the strong one, not letting go, being in control, that it's hard for you to admit you need him."

"Well thank you, Dr. Freud, for your analysis," said Maggie.

"What a sensitive and brilliant thing for a straight man to say," said Wes. "He is absolutely fucking right, Margaret. You don't have to spend the rest of your life bed-hopping. No offense, Ted."

"None taken," said Ted. "I just think if Maggie's never fallen out of love with Dave, it's ok to admit it."

"Well, I know I never stopped loving him," said Maggie. "But I guess it's been hard to say I needed anyone except my girls, but now they're women."

"You know, there's nothing wrong with being married," said Wes. "I love it so far. Can't wait to leave for our honeymoon in Cancun next month. You straight motherfuckers take marriage for granted all the time. We just fought to finally get marriage legal and you're all divorcing everybody. Anyway, if you married Dave again, you wouldn't have to cheat on people with him."

"Marriage? I obviously fail at marriage," said Maggie. "But you boys are both right: I do always end up back in Dave's arms. Maybe it's because it is where I'm supposed to be."

"Hear, hear!" said Wes.

They all raised their coffees in the air.

LISA AND Jim sat in the waiting room of the gray-walled doctor's office nervously. A couple ten years younger sat beside them, and across the room a single woman who was ten years older. They glanced at the clocks, they glanced at their phones, they glanced at the brochure they'd been handed at the desk when they checked in. The other couple was taken to the back. They waited. The single woman patient was taken back. They waited more.

"Thank you," said Lisa, under her breath, and without looking up.

"For what?" asked Jim.

"Thank you for coming here and doing this with me," said Lisa.

"You shouldn't have to thank me, Lisa," said Jim. "We both want a baby. I feel bad that we haven't been able to conceive one on our own, and we should do whatever we can to make a family happen. It's what we both want. You don't need to thank me."

"I'm scared," she said.

"Why, honey?" asked Jim.

"It's why I haven't been asking you to come here sooner," said Lisa. "I'm just scared of what we're going to discover. What if something is wrong, and for some reason we can't have a baby. It would be devastating to find that out."

All those journal entries, she thought. *I've written and written this scene out so many times and I just don't know how it's going to end. I want it to end with a baby in my arms.* Jim took her hand.

"Knowing something for fact is going to be better than wondering and worrying," he said. "We need to find out where we are so we can figure out where we're going. I'm glad we're here. It's a first step in the journey that will hopefully end with our little family."

"I never knew you felt that way about it," said Lisa.

"We've just never really talked about it that much."

"Well one of things I realized," said Jim, "Is that we weren't talking enough. I'm not going to let that happen anymore."

"Thank you for that, too," said Lisa, and she smiled at her husband.

"Stop thanking me for things you don't need to be thanking me for," said Jim. "I loved you enough to sell all those shoes on ebay, didn't I? The new nursery is going to be so nice. One way or another, we will have our family. Ok?"

"Ok," said Lisa, smiling.

They had talked about adoption and it was an option they were both willing to consider if they couldn't conceive naturally. Egg donor, in vitro, surrogate mother, adoption, whatever it took was fine with both of them.

The nurse walked in. "Mr. and Mrs. Swain?"

And they walked back to meet the doctor at the fertility clinic.

LISA HAD set up a table for three in the bakery and made chocolate croissants from scratch. It was nice to be able to prepare something for her friends. The coffee (nothing fancy here; they'd have to settle for cream and sugar) was brewing and the smell of the baking chocolate and pastry filled the air.

Maggie and Eva walked down the street together. Though

Maggie wore a vintage faux fur coat and Eva wore a modern black one with clean lines, they were bundled in practically matching hats and gloves and scarves; Lisa knew the knit shop a few blocks over where the items had been made; she was a fan as well.

They opened the door, bringing in a whoosh of cold winter air. As she hugged the other two women she could feel the cold rise off their skin and clothing. Good mornings were wished all around. Lisa's bakery had a small fireplace; it was gas and not as quaint as a wood burning fireplace, but it did the trick, and the women gathered around it, waiting to take off coats until the worst of the chill was off their bodies.

"So what's going on with Stanley and Zarina?" asked Lisa.

"Kate called me," said Maggie. "Apparently after being inspired by the glorious gay wedding on New Year's Eve, the two of them went to Vegas and eloped."

"Oh my God!" said Lisa.

"They're adorable," said Eva. "I'm so happy for them. Let's surprise them with a little shower when they get back."

"Definitely," said Lisa. "I have to ask: did Zarina ever find out about you and her mom?"

"Nah, we decided it could just be too much emotionally for her, so neither of us said anything," said Maggie.

"So you gave up our dead sluts book club, huh?" Eva asked Maggie.

"I never meant for the whole thing to turn into such a

depressing monthly chore, for shit's sake," said Maggie. "I just can't believe how far our society *hasn't* come in dealing with women having affairs."

The women took off coats, fixed their coffees and took seats by the fire.

"When a man is cheating on a woman, he has a mistress," said Eva. "When a woman is cheating on a man, she has a…a what? A mister? There isn't even a word for it."

"I read an article online at a women's health website that referred to it as 'affair partner,'" said Lisa, and the other women laughed as Lisa pulled out her perpetually present and well-worn journal.

"Well this month I did actually find a modern book about affairs, because I was trying to learn about myself and why I have been unfaithful over the years," said Maggie, taking out her copy of the book and turning to a dog-eared page. "It's not a novel and no women off themselves. Imagine that. It's called *When Good People Have Affairs*, and the author Mira Kirshenbaum writes,

'When a man cheats, he's living up to the image of untrustworthy horndog; when a woman cheats, she's betraying the idea that women are intrinsically faithful. Clearly, neither stereotype is true.'"

Lisa read the notes from the women's health article.

"79 percent of women said having an affair with a taken man was never acceptable, a surprising 46 percent admitted to having done it--and more than half said they felt no regrets. When asked whether she'd rather be a mistress or a deceived wife, more than 62 percent opted for the former, saying the forbidden fling wasn't part of a scheme to snag a husband and that they had no desire to marry the guy."

"Well look at you two," said Eva. "I was watching sappy movies and drinking wine and collecting sea glass, but I'm glad my fellow Scarlet Letter Society members have all been doing research!"

"You know, now that you're divorced, you're not technically cheating on anyone unless you count cheating on Ron and Charles with each other," observed Maggie.

"And news flash: Ron and I are over. Fun while it lasted, time for both of us to move on. No hard feelings. He got a job at another firm. So wait, are you trying to throw me out of the Scarlet Letter Society, Margaret?" said Eva, smiling.

"Of course not," said Maggie. "Once you've been branded, you've been branded. There are two types of women: those who have cheated, and those who haven't. And once you have become a wearer of the proverbial scarlet letter, there's no going back to the other side, even if you never cheat again."

"What about you?" asked Eva. "I can barely seem to keep up with your life and 'who's zooming who' as Aretha so charmingly called it."

"It's actually become surprisingly simplified. I'm too old for this shit. Ted is leaving to go be a rock star," said Maggie. "So I guess we won't be seeing each other again since he'll be in Nashville."

"Wow," said Lisa. "That is big news. What about Kate?"

"I like Kate," said Maggie, and they all laughed. "But I'm not sure about a serious ongoing relationship. I was bi-curious, obviously, though I can't say I even knew I was, but I don't really know what that road holds for me if anything in the future. Of course as we all know I remain open-minded about it. You never know."

"So wait a minute," Eva said. "If you aren't a fake lesbian anymore, Ted is taking off, and your divorce to #2 is finally final, then who the hell are you cheating on, Maggie? Maybe we should throw you out of the Scarlet Letter Society, too, ya big hypocrite."

"Oh, fuck you," said Maggie. "I'm just tired, that's all. My love life has been quite a damn rollercoaster and I sort of feel like the ride's been great, but I want to get off."

"Oh you've gotten off all right," said Eva, laughing.

"What about Dave?" Lisa asked Maggie.

"Dave," said Maggie. Her eyes seemed far away for a moment. "The only guy I've never stopped fucking."

"The only guy you've never stopped loving, too?" asked Lisa.

"Yeah, that too," said Maggie. "Though for some reason it wasn't easy for me to admit it. When I was back in the house over Christmas and the four of us were together at the breakfast table, I felt like I was home. I hadn't felt that way in a long, long time."

"You know what the bitch in the sparkly red shoes says,"

said Eva. "There's no place like home."

"That's so true," said Lisa, smiling. "And I'm happy to say I'm no longer an owner of any sparkly red shoes."

"And, what about you, Junior SLS member?" asked Maggie. "If technically Eva and I are entering the 'Wild Oats Already Sown' stage of our lives, it would leave you as the only active member of the club."

"Yeah, I should get you two a couple of Clappers and some Geritol for sure," said Lisa. Then she thought for a minute. "Being the sole wearer of the scarlet letter sounds like a lonely place to be."

"For women who cheat on their husbands, it *is* a lonely place," said Maggie. "If you don't know anyone else who has cheated, it's not like you can go to some Facebook fan page and find a bunch of other cheating women to hang around and discuss your feelings with."

"I have a confession to make," said Lisa. "You two aren't the only ones who feel like you don't belong in this club. I never did. I never slept with Ben. I only kissed him, and that was only recently. I lied to you, and I am really, really sorry."

Maggie and Eva looked at each other as though to do a quick assessment of how to handle this odd and shocking news.

Maggie couldn't help but laugh: lying seemed so out of character for Lisa. "Secret club breach! Alert the society police!" she said, chuckling.

"Why?" said Eva.

"When I met the two of you, I wanted so badly to cheat on Jim with Ben," said Lisa. "I thought maybe I could learn from you how you did it. But then, I couldn't do it. I just decided not to go down that road, because I knew there was no turning back. If I had a membership card in my purse, I would hand it back."

"Nah," said Maggie. "I think we can accept you as an honorary member, especially when we're not even going to technically be members ourselves anymore."

"Things have changed for me. Jim and I went to fertility treatment," said Lisa. "And he started seeing a therapist about his foot fetish so he could stop driving me nuts with the shoe shit. He sold the shoes and painted the shoe room with hopes it will eventually be a nursery. I have been much happier at home. I don't feel like I just want to leave anymore, I feel like I want to stay. I want a baby. I want a family. Those are the things that are important to me."

"Hang on a second," said Eva, smiling. "The three of us are the worst red A-club ever. Our Hussy of the Month club cards- *expired? Invalidated?* This is madness."

"Well, who needs a club?" said Maggie. "We know we're all bonded by our common choices, our histories, our ..."

"Our sex drives?" asked Eva, smirking.

"Yeah, I guess so," said Maggie.

"Our passion in life," said Lisa.

"Yes," said Maggie. "That's more it. We're the kind of women who need the strongest kind of men. Men who can be there without making us feel like we need them there. Who allow the independence they know we want and are secure enough to not feel threatened when we stray."

"It's not about them," said Eva. "When we cheat. I never blamed Joe. When people cheat on each other, it could be said it's 'both their faults' because it means they weren't happy in the first place, but it's always a choice."

"It's a choice," said Lisa.

"You make the choice to cheat because you're coming from a place of unhappiness," said Maggie. "It's not to hurt the other person, even a person you love. It's because you're trying to find yourself, as selfish as that may sound. But you can't walk around lost."

"It's true," said Eva. "Somehow you were not getting what you needed, so you can go out looking for it all you want, but you have to eventually find it within yourself, not with some guy."

"Do you miss them?" asked Lisa to Maggie and Eva. "Ted? Ron? Do you miss them when they aren't in your life anymore?"

"You have to be thankful for the time you had with them," said Maggie. "No reason for regrets, because it's part of who you are now. It's all about finding happiness when you figure out what that means for you, and holding on to memories, but what's that saying, about letting some things fall apart so that better things come together."

"Oh no," said Eva. "I feel like you're about to go Dr.

Seuss on us. She's right, though. I don't think there is any reason to beat ourselves up about it. Guilt is something we're taught, and something we have to unlearn. Go ahead Maggie, something about being happy or sad it's over or something?'

"Don't cry because it's over," said Maggie, making air quotes in the air. "Smile because it happened."

"Says the good doctor," said Lisa, jotting the quote down in her faithful journal.

February 2013

"Now the miles stretch out behind me,
Loves that I have lost;
Broken hearts lie victims of the game.
Then good luck, it finally struck
Like lightning from the blue:
Every highway leading me back to you."
- "The Search is Over," Survivor

The So-Called Scarlet Letter Society
Can Meet Wherever
And Whenever
They Damn Well Please

We can talk about future 'meetings,' though they will really be
get-togethers, and no longer called meetings. Casual coffees,

gatherings of friends. No more invitations, no more books (sorry, Eva!) unless they're random ones we genuinely find, love and share. Our passports into regions where most women dare not tread have been stamped, and now we're home.

from: **Ben** bnidale@starfishdesign.com
to: **Lisa** lswain@blackbirdspie.com

date: Monday, January 28, 2012, 8:41 AM
subject: excuses

> Our kiss both took me off guard and was at the same time one of the most incredible things ever to happen to me. We're not professionally involved anymore, so I can tell you I've been attracted to you since we met. My only fear is not having an excuse to see you again, short of simply wanting to repeat the magic of that kiss.
>
> Ben

Lisa sat at her bakery counter. She breathed in the smell of the raspberry tart cooking in the oven. The fire warmed the shop for customers who took the time to stop by during their busy days. She smiled at the email from Ben; that old excitement of seeing his name in her inbox was still there, though different now.

She stared at her screen. Here was her choice, in a simple email before her. Thanks to modern technology, she didn't have to endure awkward, drawn-out in-person scenes of rejections or goodbyes or temptations; she could simply hit reply.

from: **Lisa** lswain@blackbirdspie.com
to: **Ben** bnidale@starfishdesign.com

date: Monday, January 28, 2012, 9:07 AM
subject: Moments

> I agree there was magic in the kiss, but
> I am afraid I can't let it happen again.
> My devotion to my husband and my
> commitment to making my marriage
> work despite its challenges won't allow
> it, and I know you understand. But I
> want you to know that I appreciate how
> beautiful you made me feel in the time I
> knew you. Thank you for that.
> Wishing you all the best,
> Lisa

Lisa closed her laptop a tiny bit too forcefully, as if the action was closing the door on a part of her life that she wasn't 100% sure she wanted closed. As if the decisive snapping sound would convince her she was making the right choice. She had actually considered, for a significant part of the last year, sleeping with Ben. She knew it wasn't fair to him, but one of the reasons she'd considered it was the hope that she might get pregnant.

To this day, there had been no evidence that Jim was the cause of her infertility. Her own doctor had not found anything wrong with her, but neither had a doctor found something out of place with him. They were waiting for the most recent test results. But somehow Lisa had thought if she'd slept with Ben, she'd get pregnant and have some kind of secret love child; a secret she'd keep for a lifetime from Jim. She now realized that this childish fantasy could have created a lifetime of heartache and shame for not only her but potentially everyone around her.

Maybe now, with her heart set and her mind clear, her body would allow her, finally, to conceive and carry the child that would make her a mother. In a family that included a husband who loved her. Not a perfect husband, but one who loved her the best he could.

And she vowed to herself to try to do the best she could to love him back.

Eva sorted sea glass at the cottage on Matthew's Island. The collecting of the glass, finding a perfectly smooth piece in an unusual color, was the most enjoyable part of sea glass hunting, but the sorting was somehow therapeutic as well. She normally placed her day's finds of colored glass into a huge vintage metal washtub, but sorting it by color into big glass jars had a calming effect on her. *Green goes in the green jar, blue goes in the blue jar.* Her mind could wander as she did the mindless task. The whole act of sea glass hunting was soothingly ritualistic. Check the low tide chart. Go to the beach. Pick up the pieces of glass, place them into a bag. Return to the cottage, rinse off the glass. Place the glass out on the deck to dry. Put it in the large container. And then, when you had time, you sorted it.

White and green and brown were the most common colors. She only picked them up now off the beach if they were special in some way, a fragment of a written word, a perfectly tumbled piece, a complete bottle top. It was the rare colors she wanted: the cobalt blue, the Coca Cola bottle turquoise, the deep jade, the softer cornflower blue. And the rarest: the purple, the yellow, the pink, the red. The red was the holy grail. Well, technically the *orange* was the holy grail, but she had rarely known orange to be found on the island. She had only a few pieces of red after years of collecting, along with a collection of other unusual finds: a cat-eye marble, perfectly tumbled. A gorgeous aqua bottle stopper. A tiny porcelain doll's head. A few colored beads.

You never knew what you were going to find. There were pieces of a 19th century Blue Willow patterned dish that she'd found periodically over time. She'd collected so many pieces she could almost put the dish back together like a puzzle again. She'd find a piece one day and then, a month later, another piece from the same dish. It was romantic to think about where the pieces came from—a shipwreck, a long-ago ferry to Baltimore. There never seemed to be a rhyme or reason to the patterns of the tide and how the bay churned out what it churned out. But somehow, it always kept you coming back. It was so easy to forget the rest of the world when she hunted for sea glass. There was only the search to find the next piece.

Eva's phone rang. So few people called her anymore (her teenage boys always texted). It startled her, and she jumped at the sound of her own ringtone.

She looked at the phone and saw Charles's name. He knew she was at the cottage and it was safe to call. In times past, they'd only spoken when she'd been in New York.

"Hello," she said.

"Madame Eva, pretty girl," said Charles. "How are you this weekend?"

"I'm well," said Eva, looking around her at the sea glass spread around the floor and table. "And how are you, my fine French chef lover?"

"I'm better now to hear your voice," said Charles.

"That is very lovely," said Eva. "Thank you."

"I just called to tell you that I am happy you are coming to New York this week," he said. "And that I miss you, and I think of you often when you are away."

Eva felt her heart swell with emotion.

"I don't even know what to say," said Eva. "That means

a lot to me. I think of you when we're apart, too. And I miss you, too."

They chatted for awhile about work and her boys and when they would see each other again, and wished each other farewell until the next time.

This conversation was one of very few in which they'd discussed any sort of feelings with each other outside the context of passion's embrace. He wasn't the kind of guy who would use words to tell her how he felt. She was touched by the gesture of the simple phone call: he was thinking of her. It was generally understood that they saw each other when they saw each other, and they were apart when they were apart. It was nice to feel the same sort of happiness, only from a distance.

As she hung up the phone, she had mixed feelings. She did not want to need a man. She let Ron go, because it was time. Her marriage had ended, because it was time. Her life was much simpler now. She wanted it simpler. She worked, she spent time with her boys. She spent time at the cottage. She did not want to leap from the embrace of one man to the embrace of another.

She wanted to be alone, to learn to live on her own in four walls to herself at the times when her sons were not with her. *Am I in love with Charles?* she wondered, and she did not know what the future held for them. Being in love made you vulnerable to being hurt, and Eva did not like to feel vulnerable. But he was there. He'd always be there, in New

York. She knew he'd never move, and she wasn't sure she'd want him to. She didn't know how much longer she'd travel to the firm in New York. She had enough control over her career to do what she wanted, including ending it altogether. Washington? New York? She could choose one if she really wanted to; she'd tell her partners she didn't want to travel so much because of the boys. She'd use her savings and live a simple life at the cottage. But if Charles wasn't in her life anymore, she would miss him. She allowed herself to admit it. And she would be so happy for him to visit the cottage.

Maybe a weekend here with Charles, she thought, filled with the magic of the brilliant, gorgeous sunsets, crabs freshly caught from the bay, the dark, moonlit nights where you could lie on the dock and watch shooting stars...maybe that would be what they needed to fill the emptiness in their lives. *Or maybe I can just enjoy those things all by myself.*

For now, there were piles of sea glass to sort into their places, because each weathered piece, tumbled in the sands of time to perfection, had a place where it belonged.

MAGGIE PARKED her car in front of the stone Victorian house where she had raised her two grown daughters, and where she had lost her only son. She breathed out, fighting the memory of rocking her baby boy in that very porch rocker, begging God to let her son live, and later cursing that same God who did not.

I will not let the ghosts of my past affect the reality and importance of my future, she decided. Dave had invited her to dinner. He loved to cook and she did not, so she was happy for the invitation. Her mind wandered back for a moment to one of her earliest memories: her mother, curled up with her in bed under the shabby covers had said, *"I want better for you."*

He opened the door and looked at her. In his eyes, even behind his glasses, she could tell he was happy to see her. He stepped outside, and they hugged on the porch. This porch, with its history of scraped knees being bandaged, Christmas cards coming and going from the mailbox, girls playing with Barbie dolls on long ago hot summer days.

"I'm happy you're here," said Dave.

"Well, it's nice to come out to the country for a break from the big city," she said, and they laughed, because the house, in a row of Victorians on the outskirts of town, was only 12 blocks away from her own downtown shop and apartment. She'd never wandered very far from home.

"How's work?" she asked, knowing the answer.

"Just trying to keep up an old building or two," he answered.

"If anyone can do that, you can," she told him.

"I hope you're hungry," said Dave, glancing at his watch. It wasn't 6 pm yet, but Maggie was always hungry early. The *Lady is a Tramp* Frank Sinatra song line "she gets too hungry for dinner at eight" was one they'd always jokingly referenced over the years. *Who can wait until 8:00 at night for dinner?* Maggie always said. *I want to be* asleep *by then.*

She fought the urge to feel awkward in a house that used to be hers many years before. Of course, Dave had bought out her interest in the house during the divorce, and she couldn't help but feel like a visitor, despite the vase on the stone mantel she'd picked out at a fairgrounds auction forever ago and left because it went there so perfectly, despite the linens in the linen closet she'd gotten at an antique shop for their first dinner party, despite the years she had spent in that kitchen making peanut butter and jelly for girls who have been old enough for many years now to make sandwiches for themselves.

He could sense her awkwardness.

He put his arms around her. She let herself melt into the warmth of his embrace. He'd always been there for her; this hug had been something she had taken for granted. Tough as she seemed to others, in her heart she knew she'd be a mess if she didn't have Dave's arms waiting for her. Could she live on her own? Of course she could, and had for years.

But there was needing, and there was wanting, and although maybe Maggie didn't *need* to be with anyone, at the end of the day, she knew she preferred it. She wanted to feel the safety of those strong arms, even if it meant admitting she wasn't always the strongest person herself.

"It doesn't make me weak to need you," she said suddenly. He pulled away from her a bit to look down into her eyes.

"What?" Dave said, and he smiled at her.

"Anyway, it isn't really that I need you. It's that I want you, and there's a difference," said Maggie, as though trying to convince herself.

"Maggie, I have always needed you," said Dave. "I don't care who hears me admit it. It's true."

"I have always needed you, too," said Maggie. "I think I've just had a hard time admitting it."

Dave took her by the hand and led her to the kitchen. He handed her a beer, and opened one for himself.

"Want to pick a Pandora station?" he asked.

"Do you even have to ask?" she said.

"Not really," Dave said. "Soft hits of the 70s. I'd put money on it."

"No one loves the Air Supply and the Dr. Hook and the Bee Gees like I do," said Maggie.

"I know," said Dave.

"You're the Biggest Part of Me" by Ambrosia began to play. She walked around the kitchen counter, took her life's love into her arms, and they began to dance.

And in the morning, he brought her coffee in bed.

The End

ACKNOWLEDGEMENTS

Thanks first to my publisher Jason Pinter at Polis Books, for taking a chance on me when the "traditional houses" rejected the manuscript.

Thanks to my literary agent Myrsini Stephanides of Carol Mann Agency in New York, for making my dream of having a literary agent in New York come true, and for believing in me. Also to Lydia, for opening the book proposal from the slush pile and saying "oh my God" sufficiently enough to warrant interest.

To my teachers: there is no greater gift than a love for learning.

To Beth Werrell, my writing coach and friend, whose early read of the novel served to make it better. Thanks!

To Russ Smith, the publisher of SpliceToday.com where I've worked as Senior Editor for the last few years. Thank you for paying me so I had money to rent the writing cottage where the novel was written, but far more importantly, thank you for making me a better writer.

Ah, Tilghman. Thanks to the Tilghman family who provided a writing retreat where the idea for the novel began and grew, to Patricia and John at the Tilghman Island Country Store for their friendship and support and cheesesteaks, and to Jacque and Pat at Tilghman Landing, who provided the serene island spot where the book was completed.

To my beloved Tilghman Island Book Club, whose love and support is unwavering and much appreciated. "Reading Between the Wines" (even though I'm usually the one who hasn't read the book and brings Jack Daniels to meetings because I don't drink wine) has been such a nurturing environment; you ladies rock.

To Zack, Brahm, Michael and Alfie, for inspiration.

Liz, Susan, Stefanie, Cara, Patricia, Mindie, Alex, Kellen, Laura, Kara, Charlotte, Lauren, Lynne, Tracy…thank you for your friendship.

To my readers: whether you read my *Quite Contrary* newspaper columns two decades ago, my PajamasandCoffee.com blog, my Splice articles or anything in-between, I appreciate you more than I can say. You're why I'm here. Thanks for taking the time to read my words.

Finally: to my family. I was going to try to use that term to include *everyone* in my family, but my brother John fought for our country twice in Iraq and I want to be sure to avoid what we lovingly refer to as "the freedom speech" if he wasn't mentioned. So John, thanks for the freedom and for being a hero.

Much love to my amazing dad and my siblings Alex, Emily, and Drew. Beth, I miss you, thanks for always being my best cheerleader. Love you always.

I also want to thank my fantastic mom, the poet Ellie

LeJeune, for the reverend's words at the wedding. They are from her poem "Marriage Blessing" which appears in her book of poetry *Silent Song*.

To my loving husband Bob and four amazing children Sarah, Molly, Faith and Bobby: I love you beyond words. Thank you for being my team, and the heart of my world.

ABOUT THE AUTHOR

Mary T. McCarthy has been a professional journalist for over twenty years for newspapers, magazines and the Internet. *The Scarlet Letter Society* is her first novel. After completing her second novel, *The Scarlet Letter Scandal*, she has been working on a third novel to complete her trilogy: *The Scarlet Letter Storm*. She lives on Maryland's Eastern Shore with her husband and four children. Find her online at pajamasandcoffee.com or on Twitter @marymac.

Read on for an exclusive excerpt from
The Scarlet Letter Scandal

Coming soon from Mary T. McCarthy

Chapter One

"He wouldn't know a clit if it slapped him in the face," Kellie whispered, tossing her long, flat-ironed ombre hair over her shoulder.

"Well he clearly hasn't been slapped by enough of them, then," said Rachel.

"It's mortifying even listening to the two of you," said Jeannie, entering the dining room and placing a crystal cream and sugar set on the table. "Can we please change the subject?"

"Isn't some sex scandal the reason you called us over here in the first place when it's not the first Tuesday of the month?' asked Kellie, spooning what she knew was locally grown, organic fruit onto her plate.

Jeannie placed a slice of the homemade gluten-free banana walnut bread she'd made that morning onto an antique plate, returning from the sideboard in the formal dining room to seat herself beside the two other women.

"Yes, what's the story?" asked Rachel, sipping her coffee while gingerly holding the fragile cup and saucer. The eager grin lit up her pale freckled face, framed as it was by a mop of bright orange curls.

Jeannie sighed audibly and cleared her throat.

"I asked you here because as I said in the email I wanted to have a quick meeting of our Housewarming Club. I'm sorry Lisa Swain couldn't make it, something about a wedding cake." Jeannie sipped her coffee, pausing to relish in the attention of her neighbors. "But this online Internet thing is really an unbelievable story. It came across my desk and I just had to speak with someone about it right away," she said, concerned and almost bewildered. She wore a lavender twin cardigan set despite the summer heat.

"So, spill it," said Rachel. "I can't imagine what in our housewarming welcome baskets could need immediate deliberation, so it's clearly the other story you're ready to tell."

"My sister, who spends a lot of time on the Internet, said she found this, and she's all the way up in Maine!" said Jeannie, and she passed out copies of a printed blog post. "I'll give you a minute to read it."

The top of the piece of printer paper displayed the blog's logo, "The Keytown Mouse," depicting a mischievous-looking cartoon mouse nibbling on the edge of their own town's flag.

Friday, June 28, 2013
posted by F. Ritchie

Once again in our town there are stories of scandalous love affairs and clandestine secret meetings - right here in lil old Keytown! While rumors of the alleged suburban sex club ring in a certain local subdivision have not been substantiated (yet!), this blogger has been made aware of much ado right here in the downtown historic district.

According to a local source, there has been a monthly meeting taking place in the wee dawn hours at a coffee shop in downtown Keytown. Several women, including two who own shops here in town, have taken part in some type of Cheaters' Club breakfast meeting once a month for possibly years. Sources say at least three women, a formally dressed woman who doesn't appear to work in town and two women who can walk to the nearby Zoomdweebies Café from their own shops (one of which may or may not be some kind of restaurant... or maybe a bakery?), meet regularly to discuss their sexcapades. A flyer spotted in the bookstore/ coffee shop trash can refers to them as "The Scarlet Letter Society." The café even opens early to accommodate these private meetings - no word on whether shop owner Zarina Harandi is a member of the clandestine club. Stay tuned for more details.

As usual, the Keytown mouse you don't even see hiding in the corner hears everything.

"Well holy shit and hot damn!" exclaimed Kellie, not noticing as Jeannie pursed her lips. "This is hilarious! Who is this F. Ritchie mouse person, anyway? Seriously, there are still gossip columns?"

"The whole Internet is a gossip column," said Rachel, wryly. "It doesn't surprise me at all that there is kinky shit going on around us."

"I for one am surprised," said Jeannie, standing, as a blush crept up around her neck. Her brown eyes and brown hair were ordinary: a neat bobbed haircut framed her alarmed face, and she had applied a bit of mascara and lip gloss for the occasion.

"I don't even know what a sex club ring is and I can't even fathom that there are women who do nothing but sit around all day gossiping about their trampy sex lives," Jeannie continued. "I hope these women don't have children. The poor things. This is what's wrong with our society. That promiscuous women like these are out there cheating on their husbands and being home wreckers while the rest of us are trying to raise our children with decent morals and values in this community."

Straightening her knee-length navy skirt, Jeannie sat down with a huff after finishing her stump speech and refilling her decaf coffee. She reached up to pat down her already perfectly coiffed hair.

Kellie and Rachel gave each other sidelong glances,

seemingly to decide who would respond to the outburst first. They knew as a churchgoing, full time stay-at-home mom and President of the elementary school PTA (not to mention the wife of homeowners' association President), Jeannie took issues like these seriously. Perhaps more seriously than most.

"Who knows if it's even true?" suggested Rachel. "At least three-quarters of what we find on the Internet is a lie, I'm sure." She smiled helpfully in Jeannie's direction, helping herself to another piece of banana bread.

"And not to be argumentative, but is it really even any of our business who's doing what in the bedrooms and coffee shops of this town?" Kellie smiled to lighten the mood, but she wasn't inclined to be overly accommodating of Jeannie's rant. At 32 and the youngest of the trio, Kellie was divorced, and engaged to a man she'd met while still married. She had volunteered for the housewarming committee at the homeowners' association, thinking it meant she'd get to deliver welcome baskets to new moms or new neighbors. She was surprised to realize the homeowners' association operated as some kind of vigilante self-policing McMafia, enforcing ordinances about landscaping violations and bickering over boats parked in driveways.

Jeannie put down her coffee, delivering an icy stare in Kellie's direction.

"This neighborhood, which my husband Chaz selflessly donates his volunteer time to help manage, is already under threat by reckless homeowners who have simply walked away from their mortgages and abandoned their properties, not to mention the high number of rental properties that have popped up here in Stony Mill. The last thing we need is some kind of deviant sex club, not to mention a group of harlots running around ready to steal our husbands!"

She stood and clacked her way into the kitchen, her low-heeled conservative pumps clicking on perfectly polished hardwood floors.

Rachel looked at Kellie, who raised an eyebrow and shook her head, making the circular-finger "crazy" sign with her forefinger pointing to the side of her head. Rachel nodded her head in the direction of the large portrait of Jesus hanging over the dining room sideboard. The Lord, bedecked in a white robe and pleasant half-smile, sat at what appeared to be a news desk, his eyes seemingly following you wherever you went in the room. She made a quick but mocking sign of the cross, folding her hands in pantomimed prayer, which caused Kellie to accidentally laugh out loud.

Jeannie walked back in.

"Is something funny?" she asked.

"No, sorry, Jeannie, I was just laughing at how clumsy I am getting crumbs all over my lap," said Kellie, blushing and dusting imaginary crumbs from her black yoga pants.

"Who else have you talked to about this?" asked Rachel.

"Only the two of you so far," said Jeannie. "I was going to mention it at my church book club tonight. I'm sure they will want to say a prayer for these sinners all around us."

"Oh I'm sure you'll find some sympathetic ears there," said Rachel. "I don't spend too much time on the Internet when I'm at the accounting firm, but when I get back to the office I'm going to check out this Keytown Mouse and see if I can find any clues about who's writing it."

Jeannie brought the coffee pot over to the table, but the other women refused another cup.

"Did you want to cover anything we can do to help with the neighborhood welcome baskets?" asked Kellie, unconsciously straightening up a bit in her chair.

"Well, with all of this hubbub I had forgotten to bring it up," said Jeannie. "Lisa Swain has volunteered to donate muffins from her bakery in town for the baskets. She can't usually make meetings because of her shop schedule but she's willing to drop them off."

"That's great," said Kellie, happy to change the subject. "Lynette over on Oak Street has offered to provide some of her Mary Kay samples, and I was going to ask a few shops in downtown Keytown for coupons."

"I could help with that too," said Rachel. "I see Lisa in town all the time since my office is near her bakery. I could offer to pick up muffins and put some feelers out around town for coupons too."

"Restaurants... bakeries..." said Jeannie, distracted, glancing down at the blog post on the printed page. "Hmm, I wonder which one of these downtown places are home to the "Scarlet Letter Society" members?"

Kellie stood. "Could be anyone. You just never know with people these days. Well, I have a yoga class to teach so I'd better run."

Taking the welcome excuse to depart, Rachel stood as well. She unconsciously straightened her slightly wrinkled celery green Banana Republic dress. What was it about being in Jeannie's house that kept making her feel like she needed to straighten something? "Yes, I need to get into the office. So many people filed late tax extensions this year."

Clearly not wanting to be the only one who didn't have something busy to do, Jeannie noted, "Yes, well the PTA meeting is coming up and I need to get over to the school to help change bulletin boards and work on that meeting agenda." She glanced at her watch and escorted them to the door, offering a tight smile. "See you next time, ladies."

Rachel and Kellie walked down the driveway. Sporting the Adidas yoga outfit that had made her feel underdressed, Kellie glanced at Jeannie's perfectly manicured lawn and professionally edged sidewalk. There wasn't a weed to be seen, not even in the mulched flower area around the mailbox. Kellie thought about the crab grass and dandelions in her own yard, and the weeds in the flower containers beside her front door.

"Why do I feel like we just got dismissed from the principal's office?" Rachel asked her.

"I don't know," said Kellie. "I don't mean to talk about her behind her back but she sure has that way about her, doesn't she?"

"It must be a heavy burden to be completely perfect," said Rachel, shifting in her dress, a hand automatically moving to try to control her disheveled ginger curls. "I wouldn't know."

"Me either," said Kellie.

"So we'll have to continue our earlier conversation later I guess?" said Rachel. "I definitely didn't mean for her to overhear us."

"Ya think?" said Kellie. "I was totally horrified. The last thing I would talk about in front of the queen of the subdivision is my sex life!"

"Especially if she knew it may or may not have been her own husband you were talking about in that clit comment, right?" asked Rachel knowingly of her younger neighbor.

Kellie made the "shoot me" motion, pointing a finger-gun at her head.

"That would go over about as well as if she knew I had fake tits," said Kellie. "And *who even uses* the word harlot?" she asked, giggling. She waved and started jogging toward her side of the neighborhood.

As Rachel got in her car and pulled away, she glanced back at the beige vinyl-sided former model home and noticed Jeannie lowering the curtain she'd been holding aside to look outside, ever watchful of her neighbors.

KELLIE SLOWED her pace to walk past the matching pair of

large faux landscaping rocks on either side of the walkway to her house, which was a slightly darker shade of beige than Jeannie's, only two streets away. She stopped to deadhead a few geraniums and pull a few weeds from the antique black urns on either side of the red-painted door. She had gone to Home Depot one day and bought a can of red paint, applying it simply so she could tell people "it's the one with the red door" when they entered her subdivision maze where the houses all look the same.

She walked into her house, closed the door behind her and exhaled briskly, literally blowing off the feeling of negativity that clung to her from the visit to Jeannie's house. *How did I manage to get myself into a situation where I have to deal with* her? She thought, as she tried to brain-bleach the newscaster Jesus' roaming stare. She shook out her arms, another effort to shed the puritanical vibes she felt like she'd been exposed to. She busied herself straightening the place, grabbing shoes off the floor and putting them in the closet, placing the morning dishes in the dishwasher, wiping down the counters. She glanced at the time on her phone. Her clients would be there shortly for what was known as the Wednesday "Hump Day Nooners" club.

Clients came and went from the house daily. She placed "Kellie Muller, Licensed Personal Trainer" ads for her fitness and yoga classes in the local paper where everyone could see the legitimacy of her home business. She had applied for and received the necessary home business permits; the paperwork describing her renovated full basement included architectural plans showing the weights, hardwood floor yoga area, two spin machines and two treadmills.

But none of it was there.

The door to the fully renovated basement was locked at all times, a digital combination on the lock to the interior door leading downstairs and a similar digital lock on the exterior entrance where cellar steps led to the large space and its individual rooms.

Kellie climbed the stairs to her second floor master suite. Another digital lock on the door here. She liked her privacy. She quickly entered the password on the keypad and went into the room, pulling her yoga top off. She looked up just before she ran into her fiancée, Brandon, who was standing before her completely naked. He smiled at her, stroking his erect penis.

"Heard you come in. I want to fuck you before the Nooners club gets here," he said, hunger in his gaze.

"Fair enough, sexy," said Kellie, stepping out of her black yoga pants. She walked over to the door between their small sitting room and the bedroom. Hanging above the doorway was a metal bar designed for pull-ups and rarely used exclusively for traditional exercise. Brandon walked up behind her, pressing against her naked, shapely ass so she could feel exactly how interested he was.

She turned to face him, opening her mouth for a long, tongue-probing kiss. Her hands raked through his mop-top dirty blond hair and she dragged her fingernails down the sides of his rippled abs and around to his ass, where she squeezed both cheeks.

"But we don't have much time."

"They know the combination to the outside entrance downstairs," said Brandon. "They'll wait." He reached down and picked up two ankle braces with hooks on them, looking at her inquisitively.

Kellie smiled her approval, lowering herself the floor, leaning back on her elbows and extending her feet to Brandon. He attached the foot cuffs, clasping two buckles on the sides of each ankle. While her legs were spread, he lowered his head and gave slow, teasing licks to her most sensitive place, running his hands lightly down the sides of her thighs, raising goosebumps and sending chills up her spine.

She breathed in the smell of the sandalwood aftershave he used and her nipples hardened in anticipation of what was to come. He caressed the aroused peaks of her breasts with his strong thumbs, following the motion with his mouth and tongue. She reached down and took him into her hands as he moaned with pleasure.

He stood up, taking her right foot in his hands and raising the hook to attach it to the metal bar, which she noticed he'd adjusted so it was about a third of the way down from the top of the doorway. A notch in the doorway marked the spot where the bar had been before. He raised her left foot and clicked the second hook into place. She could freely move her feet from side to side because he hadn't attached the brace clamps on either side that would lock her feet in place. She expertly raised the lower half of her body and grabbed the top of the bar with her hands. He massaged the center of her pleasure zone with one hand, his other hand stroking his own shaft.

Kellie arched her back, dropping her hands down to grab the corners of the doorway near the floor. She was now fully upside-down and he stood in the doorway behind her. A set of handcuffs was hung on hooks on either side of the bottom of the doorway, but there was no time for additional bondage. Brandon stroked himself just outside her wetness, entering her more deeply each time. She thrust her hips forward in anticipation. In this position, he could reach her breasts, which he massaged, licking his thumbs and running them over her nipples. Since she was in a swinging position, each time he entered her she rocked on the bar that held her feet in place. He reached around to grab her hips, holding her in place to fuck her harder until they both came — the first orgasms of the day in the house before they went downstairs to join the others who'd arrived seeking more. They caught their breath as Brandon unshackled her.

Kellie quickly cleaned up, putting on a tight white Spandex ruched dress and a pair of strappy sandals. She glanced in the mirror, touched up her hair, spritzed on some Juicy perfume and applied red lip gloss. She glanced at her phone; it was already 12:15.

Brandon, who'd thrown on a pale blue linen shirt and khaki shorts but was still barefoot, was downstairs unlocking the door to the fully furnished, customized basement that had the feel of a nightclub. Kellie caught up and they walked downstairs together, hearing voices.

Music had been turned on when someone hooked their phone up; the state-of-the-art speakers played an R&B mix from an iTunes collection. The main lounge area in the center of the room appeared like a small urban dance club. A sleek black and chrome bar was placed diagonally in one corner. The LED-lit acrylic dance floor was shaped like a hexagon, with the bar to the left and a polished brass stripper pole near the right corner. Two matching minimalist midcentury red leather sofas bracketed the dance floor. The walls and ceilings were mirrors. Behind the dance floor hung a 60-inch smart LED HDTV that was currently featuring three naked women and two men wearing nothing but cowboy hats. The sound had been turned off in favor of the music selections.

"Welcome everyone!" said Kellie. "Happy Hump Day!"

Sitting on the couch sipping Diet Cokes were The Watchers, a 40-something couple who insisted on anonymity were always referred to as "A" (the man) and "B" (the woman). They never interacted sexually with the other club members, but they loved to watch.

"Hi, Kellie," said B, crossing her legs and sitting back. "Happy Hump Day to you, too!"

Brandon walked over and poured rum and Cokes for himself and Kellie.

Near the exterior entrance to the space was a small corner kitchen area that included a refrigerator, sink, and small corner counter and cabinet. Drinks, fruit and other food items were provided, and a glass bowl on the counter collected soda and snack money.

The name of the secret suburban sex club was Rocks, chosen for its multiple meanings. Swingers in the neighborhood always had landscaping rocks at the ends of their driveways, indicating a willingness to engage in sex with other couples. The slogan "get your rocks off" had been thrown around somewhat jokingly, and a small neon sign hanging from the ceiling near the bar read "On the Rocks."

Holding their drinks, Kellie and Brandon starting dancing when Chaka Khan's "Ain't Nobody" began to play.

"Hello, everyone," said Felicia as she and her friend Mycah beeped through the combination password and walked in. Kellie had met the twenty-something bi-curious black girls at her gym and become friends with them. One day a locker room conversation led Kellie to invite them over for a party, and they'd been club members ever since. Still wearing their gym clothes, Felicia and Mycah headed to the bathroom to shower and change.

The shower room was built of glass block and lit from the inside. Club members could see individuals or couples or threesomes who were inside the area, but only in silhouette.

The song ended and Kellie walked around the perimeter of the room, opening three closed doors to smaller rooms. "So what's everyone in the mood for today, in addition to watching these gorgeous ladies soap up each other's tits?"

She smiled to herself, thinking of the horrifying scene this morning at Jeannie's house. If only the PTA President knew how often her husband had been in these very rooms.